The Rose-Bearer

by
Lizabeth May

**LIBERTY
PRESS**

ISBN: 0-938743-05-8

For my three loves

Many thanks to:

Tom Doyal, who gave me the time, space and computer with which to begin this book, and the incentive to finish it.

Scott Winnett, who put my work through his mental shredder and made me piece it back together.

C. D. Burleson, who proofed, edited, and argued over ideas with me, and still loved me afterwards.

Jeff C., who knows why.

ABOUT THE AUTHOR

Lizabeth May graduated from Oberlin College with a major in voice and a minor in lesbianism.. She then went on to receive her master's degree from the University of Texas at Austin, while simultaneously research- ing breaking and bonding for this book. Currently she is beginning her campaign to be a famous opera singer.

Der Rosenkavalier
by Richard Strauss

The opera is set in eighteenth century Vienna and begins in the apartments of the Princess von Werdenberg (the Marschallin) while her husband is away hunting. She is being embraced by Octavian, her young lover, when there is a commotion outside the door. Octavian ducks behind a screen, and emerges in women's clothes as the Marschallin's serving girl, Mariandel. Baron von Ochs of Lerchenau enters and seeks the aid of the Marschallin in obtaining the hand of fifteen-year-old Sophie Faninal, daughter of a wealthy merchant. The Baron makes no secret of the fact that he wants her for her wealth, and no sooner spies Mariandel than he starts flirting with her and trying to seduce her.

When the Baron departs, the Marschallin asks Octavian to take a silver rose to Sophie as a token of the Baron's love. As Act I ends, the Marschallin reflects on her youth, and on her fears that the passage of time will bring her affair with Octavian to an end.

Act II begins with Sophie receiving the rose, but falling in love with its bearer, Octavian, and he with her. The Baron enters to be presented to Sophie anbd have the contract signed. She finds him boorish and lecherous, and Octavian picks a quarrel with him. They fight and Octavian wounds him in the arm. Sophie declares she will never marry the Baron, and her father, who has social ambitions, threatens to send her to a convent unless she does. Act II ends with the Baron receiving a note from Mariandel setting up a tryst.

In Act III the Baron shows up at the inn to keep the rendezvous with Mariandel. As he drinks with her, tricks are played on him: he sees faces in panels, a woman appears claiming he is her husband, children appear and call him papa. At last the police appear and charge him with leading young girls astray. He denies the charge, but his story becomes more and more muddled. Herr Faninal and Sophie appear, and Herr Faninal is furious to find the Baron in such a situation. Sophie renounces him. The Marschallin arrives and persuades the police to let the Baron go. Octavian reveals the trick by appearing in men's clothing. And creditors soon swarm around the Baron, demanding to be paid for the evening's services, bearing him off in their midst.

The Marschallin sees that Octavian and Sophie have fallen in love and urges Octavian to woo and win Sophie. She sings again of her mistreatment at the hands of time and men. Octavian and Sophie are united, and the opera ends as Octavian gives the Marschallin one last look in token of their past love.

Chapter 1

The butterflies in her stomach were right on schedule. "No matter how many thousands of auditions I sing," Suzette thought, "I still get nervous."

She worried when she wasn't nervous. If she didn't get the jitters in advance, she would invariably get nervous on stage. She could sing well enough when she wasn't cool and collected, but she wanted every performance to be perfect.

Suzette had never sung previously with the great Cosmopolitan Opera Company. She had successfully made her career elsewhere. Now that she was established, Suzette had been asked to sing for the C. O. C. Today's audition was merely a formality.

Getting out of the taxi, Suzette headed for the stage door. She kept singing her newest audition aria in her head. Using a new aria was uncomfortable, but it was from the role Suzette had been offered. *Only a masochist would enjoy an audition,* Suzette thought. *I've tied my own hands to the rack.* She shook herself and handed her music to the pianist. Smoothing the turquoise silk of her dress, she composed her thoughts and walked out into the blinding glare on the stage.

"My name is Suzette Etoile. I would like to sing 'Wie du warst! Wie du bist!' from *Der Rosenkavalier.*" Her voice sliced through the deafening silence of the theater. She dropped her hands lightly to her side as the music began. All the fleeting thoughts disappeared from her head as she prepared to sing. Every nerve in her body tingled as she expanded, filling her lungs with air, waiting for the first sounds to burst forth. Suzette no longer noticed the bright lights and the faceless forms out in the house as she began to sing. Her voice and spirit soared together into the great emptiness, filling it completely. She felt the earth pouring energy into her body, and she in turn poured it into her voice. The aria ended in minutes, but an eternity passed in silence before a disembodied voice said, gruffly, "Thank you."

She was dismissed. They didn't even ask for a second aria. Suzette thanked them and glided off the stage.

Once off stage, the stage manager came up and asked Suzette to wait, then went out into the house. Suzette collapsed in a chair. She felt drained.

Finally the stage manager returned with a note. "How about lunch?— Fred Carlsen." The casual note was so ludicrous after all the tension of the morning that Suzette laughed. "Tell him I'd... no, better take a note." She hurriedly scribbled her acceptance and was alone once more. The door to the house opened again but this time Fred Carlsen himself came through it.

"Fred!" Suzette leapt up to hug the tall man. "I saw the signature on the note, but I couldn't believe it was you. I had heard that you were in town, though. What are you doing here?"

"I'm directing *Der Rosenkavalier*."

"Directing! Good for you! Fred," Suzette exclaimed, clasping his hand warmly, "I knew we'd work together again some day. Only I thought it would be in a concert, with you at the piano. How did you wind up directing at the C.O.C.?"

Fred grinned his old Cheshire Cat grin, his grey eyes twinkling in delight. "I'll tell you all about it later. I'm hungry!"

Sitting in a posh little café half an hour later, Suzette couldn't resist peeking at Fred over her menu. She admired the familiar long nose, noting that he still had the same clear smooth skin and cute dimples. "You look like a little kid with gray hair," she remarked. "And still disgustingly thin."

"I'll take that as a compliment, thank you." He ordered a cheeseburger and a double order of fries before handing his menu back to the waitress.

"Still the same old Fred," she laughed. She ordered a shrimp salad and a croissant, then relinquished her menu as well. "You were going to tell me how you came to be the head honcho at the C.O.C."

"In a nutshell, I worked my way up through the ranks just like anybody else. I was in the right place at the right time, more than once."

Suzette was content to leave it at that. She would pick up more information later. "So I'll be singing Octavian for sure?"

"Of course! I have big plans for this production. It's going to be spectacular. The biggest one I've done." He paused to bite off a quarter of his burger.

"It has to be spectacular— it was written that way." Suzette thought for a moment about the lavish sets and costumes required for the opera. "Do you know yet what it's going to look like?"

"Are you kidding? My designers have been thinking about it for months, ever since we chose it. After lunch we can look at the designs. Rehearsals start Monday." He flagged down the waitress and ordered two hot fudge sundaes. "You do want one, don't you?"

"You're supposed to ask, *then* order. But it does sound good." Suzette indulged herself in nostalgia. "Just like we used to do at Campus Restaurant."

Fred chuckled. "And now you're Suzette Etoile. An amusing if slightly tacky stage name..."

"I thought it sounded just hokey enough to work. Quite frankly, it has."

"Ah, but when I met you you were still Susie Eton."

"*Susan* Eton."

"Come now. You were Susie to me as much as I was Freddie to you... no one would dare call me that now." Amused, Fred mopped up the last of his catsup with a thick french fry.

"I would... and I confess that Cass calls me Susie. I do still think of you as Freddie."

"What have you been doing the past ten years? I've followed your career in all the opera rags, so tell me the *real* gossip— for instance, who's Cass?"

"Who do you think? I've been living like an old married woman for the past five years. Her name is Cass— short for Cassandra. How about you?"

"You know me, I'll probably never settle down. I just seduce all the lovely young tenors that come to me to audition! Just kidding, of course." Suzette knew Fred had to at least be telling a partial truth, but couldn't admit it— not even to her, after so many years.

"So what else do you do these days besides direct operas? As if that wasn't enough?"

"Nothing, really. I have a house just outside of town, with a huge lawn and a garden. You would love my fireplace! It's about twice the size of the one in your senior dorm. And the garden is backed by a few apple trees. I'll have a good crop this year."

"I never pictured you as a farmer, Fred."

"Nor did I. But it helps me think. When I get a mental block while staging, or if I've had an argument with one of my divas, I go out and hoe corn or pick tomatoes. It's very therapeutic. And cheaper than a psychiatrist." He scraped the bottom of his sundae glass. "Let's get out of here."

4

They paid the check and walked back to Fred's car. "Would you like some help finding an apartment?" Fred asked.

"Sure. I'll have to get something right away if rehearsals start next week."

"Of course you're staying with me tonight. We'll get an early start tomorrow."

Suzette protested, then agreed. They drove back to her hotel. After paying the desk clerk, Suzette had to admit she was glad to leave. "I hate being alone at night. It isn't easy, after living with someone for so long, even if I am away from home a lot."

"Where did you meet Cass?"

"At a theater back home. I was singing Donna Elvira for fun and no profit, and she was the technical director. She works at the university there as the set designer, but this was a town production. Her *Don Giovanni* sets were amazing, especially considering the budget she had to work around. She designed the lighting for it too. You should see us together— two flaming redheads!" She shook her head as she laughed, the light catching red glints in her auburn hair. Suzette returned her attention to Fred. "I feel like I need to squeeze you again to make sure you're real."

"When you came barreling at me today in the theater, I had deja-vu. You remember that time you came back to college to visit. I had heard you were in town. But I never expected to see you run down the hall and tackle me!"

"I did, didn't I. Well, that's what you get for being cute. Beautiful women try to jump your bones."

"Unfortunately, you're not far from wrong. Margaret Byrd has been trying to get me in bed for the last two seasons. I don't think it's me. I think she's just hot for anything— she doesn't seem to be getting it at home. You'll meet her at the read-through next Monday. She's singing the Marschallin."

5

They had reached the gate. Fred stopped the car when they had entered his property. "You have to get out to fully appreciate the view."

While Suzette walked up the gravel path to admire the garden, neatly tucked into a small orchard and tied up with a pretty white fence, Fred waited, watching. He noted the years' changes in Suzette. She walked with more grace and assurance, her posture adding more height to her already tall frame. Suzette's fondness for fine dining must have been offset by exercise and hard work, for the curve of her hips to her slim waist was still as sexy as ever. When Suzette turned back toward the car, Fred could see her gamine grin, her hazel eyes flashing with pleasure.

"Thanks for letting me out, Fred. I enjoyed the little walk. Your garden is, I hate to say it, very cute, Fred. No other word can describe it!"

Suzette's face was flushed with the cold of oncoming night. Fred could see the ghosts of Suzette's old freckles rise to the surface.

"Wait till you see the house. It's just around the bend."

"It's lovely." Suzette coveted the big bay window. "I'll bet you have wonderful parties out here."

"All our cast parties are out here now. It's become quite a tradition." He unlocked the trunk. Retrieving her one small bag, Suzette walked up the front steps ahead of Fred. She stopped and looked back the way they had come.

"Well, I'm impressed. But don't get a swelled head—you have to come to Elmira and see our house."

After Suzette was settled into one of the upstairs guestrooms, they sat down to have a glass of tea. "I wish it were cold enough to build a fire."

"It might be, later. We're supposed to have a frost tonight. Which reminds me, I need to cover the garden. Care to help?"

By the time they finished, dusk was settling down around them. "I think I'm ready for that fire, whether you are or not!"

They loaded their arms with logs and went back in the house. Suzette knelt on the rough stone hearth to build the fire while Fred went for more tea.

"I noticed you aren't drinking these days," Fred remarked as he set down the glasses.

"I gave it up for Lent."

"No, seriously, I thought you'd want a beer."

"At our age I'm surprised you even ask. And you haven't imbibed any today either. But then, you never were much of a drinker." Suzette picked up the tea he had poured for her. "Drinking affects my voice. I can't think of a better reason to quit. But I do indulge at cast parties— two drinks, that's all I can have." She smiled. "Besides, Cass doesn't drink much, just on special occasions. She's been a good influence on me. I'm down to caffeine as my only drug." She waved her tea glass. "I hope you have coffee for tomorrow morning!"

"I hate the stuff myself. But I do keep a can on hand for— ahem— overnight guests."

"Do you often have these overnight guests?"

"As often as possible." They both chuckled, then fell silent.

"I'm about ready to turn in," Suzette hinted.

"Well, you know where everything is, now. Make yourself at home. I'll see you in the morning."

Suzette lay awake, staring into the darkness. She thought of Cass, who would be asleep in their bed by now. Sleeping in different beds every night kept Suzette from getting her rest. She would be glad to get an apartment of her own. She would be close enough this time for Cass to drive up on weekends, or to go home herself. The thought of Cass beside her in a new place was pleasing. Suzette drifted off to sleep, exhausted, lulled by the memory of Cass' warm scent.

The next morning, bacon and eggs had perfumed the house by the time Suzette came downstairs. *A hot shower is a good way to start the day,* she thought, *but two cups of coffee and I'll be ready for anything.*

"Good morning! Looks like we'll have a good day for house hunting."

Sunshine streamed through the kitchen windows. Suzette smiled. "I don't smell any coffee."

"I just supply it. You have to make it yourself." Fred bent down to check the biscuits. "How do you like your eggs?"

"Over easy. Where are the coffee filters?"

"Use a paper towel. They work better anyway."

After breakfast they climbed into Fred's sleek silver sportscar. They started off eagerly, but by noon their energy was flagging. "I hate looking for apartments," Suzette cried after another disappointment. "Let's go have lunch."

Spying a cool green park, complete with huge shade trees and several swingsets, Fred swung his car into a parking space. The surly man at the hotdog stand growled as he filled Suzette's request for extra mustard.

"I guess it's just not anyone's day today." Suzette sighed.

"I know what'll make us feel better. Come on," Fred said, then set off at a trot toward the swingset.

Suzette followed reluctantly, but soon they were both swinging merrily. After a while, Suzette slowed to a stop. Breathless from swinging and slightly nauseous from the hot dogs, she had to sit down on a bench. "You were right," she told Fred, "I do feel better—mentally, at least." The wave of nausea passed, and they set off again on their appointed rounds.

Again, disappointment followed disappointment. Suzette sighed as she crossed off another advertisement. "We only have three ads left," she moaned, as she surveyed the newspaper littered with red X's. They continued in silence until Fred swung into a long drive lined with trees. "At least this looks promising..."

The beautiful entrance proved to be deceptive. The manager was obviously more interested in keeping up outside appearances than in keeping up the apartments themselves. Suzette gratefully breathed the fresh autumn air as they closed the door on the stale stench of the last inhabitants' dogs. Even without the smell, the place had been a dismal failure. Small and dark, with very few windows, the apartment had boasted a forty-year-old set of kitchen appliances, leaky faucets and cracked tile in the bathroom, and a stain on the ceiling of the master bedroom that looked suspiciously like an old leak. Suzette slowly made another large red X.

"Maybe we should call it quits for today and start fresh again tomorrow," Fred kindly suggested. He hated seeing his friend looking like a whipped dog.

"But I have to find a place as soon as I can!" Suzette wailed.

"I know, but it is a lot to expect in one day."

"Let's at least look at these last two places. Then maybe we'll see some new ads in tomorrow's paper."

The next apartment had been rented the previous day. The advertisement was simply running out its time. "I'm not familiar with the next address," Fred told Suzette. "There's a map in the glove compartment." So far Fred had found the advertised apartments through his knowledge of the city.

Winding their way down a back street, Suzette began to think about Cass. *If she'd been here, perhaps we would have compromised and taken one of those other places*, she thought. *But then again, when we bought our house it had to be perfect. Maybe I'm being unreasonable in my standards—after all, it isn't as though I'm going to live there forever!*

She paused in her musings to re-read the last ad. It did sound promising, but so had the others.

> Spacious apartment; nice
> trees & neighborhood, fire-
> place, CA/CH, wash/dry; no
> children; cats welcome.
> 4905 Windham.

The part about the cats looked especially inviting.

"Here we are!" Fred's voice brought Suzette back to earth.

"But this is a house! Correction, this is a Victorian mansion! There must be some mistake."

"There's the number on the mailbox. 4905 Windham. If there is a mistake, maybe they can tell us the correct address— I'm sure they've had lots of inquiries about the ad." They parked the car on the street and walked up the long cobblestone drive. A gentleman dressed in an old but well cared-for smoking jacket answered the door.

"We've come in answer to an ad for an apartment, but the address seems to be incorrect. Perhaps you..."

The elderly gentleman interrupted her. "This is the correct address. Do come in."

"Allow us to introduce ourselves." Suzette felt a need to be slightly formal. "I am Susan Eton, and this is my friend, Fred Carlsen. May I see the apartment?"

"Right this way."

The apartment was more like a small house attached by a breezeway to the back of the main house. It had once housed the family servants, but had been totally remodeled. The downstairs walls had been removed to form a large livingroom where a small brick fireplace had been added. A wet bar stood in one corner. A narrow staircase led to the second floor which held a tiny kitchen and the bathroom of pale green tile. The staircase continued from the kitchen up to the third floor. When Suzette reached the top she was delighted to find that the whole floor was devoted to the single bedroom. Three walls were almost entirely filled with windows. Both the early morning and late afternoon sun would fill the room with welcome light. The southern window looked out upon a majestic lawn that gently sloped down into a small grove of ash trees. An ancient oak added to the foliage to complete the illusion of being isolated in the country.

Suzette was delighted. "Is it already taken?"

"No," Mr. Thayer replied. "It's been too expensive for some, and too small for others."

"The kitchen is a little small, and I can see how the stairs might become bothersome. But I have to admit, I love it. When could I move in?"

"The apartment's ready. You could move in as soon as you'd like."

They signed the papers in the main house. Mrs. Thayer brought cups of steaming tea on a silver tray. Soon they were all talking and laughing as though they were old friends.

"Good-bye, Joseph. Good-night, Irene," she sang as they left. "Thanks for everything. I'll see you tomorrow."

Chapter 2

Suzette drummed her fingers on the bedside table while she waited for her call to go through.

"Hello?"

"Collect call from Susie, will you pay?"

"Yes, of course, operator."

"Cass!"

"Hi, sweetiecakes. What's going on?"

"I have had the most incredible luck! I've found a wonderful place to live— and Fred said I couldn't do it in one day!"

"Wait— who's Fred?"

"He's the stage director at the C.O.C. You remember Fred Carlsen, my old college buddy. . ."

"How could I not remember? You're always talking about your old escapades!"

"This is not going to be another dull opera season, I can tell already. But I'll tell you more about Fred later. You must know about this adorable place we found." Suzette animatedly described the little staircase, the heavy oak mantel over the fireplace, all the little nooks and crannies. . . every detail right down to Irene's teacake.

"Sounds wonderful— when do you move in?"

"I'm going furniture shopping tomorrow and having it all delivered right away. I'll be down this weekend to get my clothes. You know, I like this place so much

I just might make it a permanent retreat! But only if you like it too," Suzette amended.

"I'd like to go back with you after you come to get your clothes. If I get all my work done Friday I can do it."

"That would be wonderful. . . better yet, why don't I just stay down there all weekend? It would be good to be home for a while. I sure do miss you, love."

"I miss you too, darling. So do Gertie and Alice. I suppose you'll be taking Gertie up there too?"

"I have to— you should know that by now. Gertie's my good luck charm. Irene and Joseph love cats, so she'll fit right in." Suzette suppressed a yawn. "I'm really tired. I'm afraid I'm about to fall asleep on the phone. I'll probably call again before I see you. Take care— I love you."

"I love you too. Good-night, darling."

Suzette gently set the receiver back in its cradle. It is so difficult to hang up, she thought sadly to herself. Suzette pictured Cass beside her, brilliant red hair fanned out into a shimmering backdrop for her face and shoulders. Cass' green eyes would smoulder and spark. Suzette mentally traced her lover's round-tipped nose, high cheekbones and strong chin. Cass would stretch her long muscular legs under the sheets, then turn and fold Suzette in her arms, their bodies almost perfectly aligned— toe to toe, thigh to thigh, breast to breast. Suzette hugged her pillow to help ease her longing for Cass. Finally exhaustion won over unfulfilled desire. Suzette let out a long sigh, almost reluctantly switching off the lamp.

The next morning was dismal. A light drizzle kept the usual hustle and bustle of the main streets down to a minimum. Suzette sailed into the furniture store, her long cape flowing gracefully about her. Nothing could dampen her spirits today. She loved to shop for furniture. Every time she moved, she sold it all and bought a new set. She claimed that the cost of moving was about what she lost every time she sold her furniture, but Cass knew the real reason. Suzette loved new furniture. It was one of her private indulgences, like keeping Gertie with her wherever she went.

Suzette always looked for sofas first. She had the whole shopping experience down to a science. The young sales assistant in the sofa section was obviously awed at the imposing figure in the dark rust colored cape. He almost tripped over his own feet as he went to offer his services.

Suzette had an eye for color and form. She admired many of the sofas, sniffing in disdain at others. She was performing for the boy— hardly 18, from his appearance— even though she had immediately spied the one she wanted. Finally she circled back to the sofa she had picked out. Dark grey trim enhanced a lavender loveseat that contained a folding bed. The art deco style appealed to her. "Have this delivered this afternoon." With that, she left the boy standing in her wake, his mouth hanging open. That done, she could build the rest of the livingroom around the loveseat.

A matching glass coffee table and end table set was the next purchase. Suzette didn't bother to make a show for the rest of the furniture store employees; she was intent on her furnishings. Everything had to be just right. Not just for appearances, but for her own sake. Singers are artists. To Suzette, furnishing an apartment was like painting a masterwork. Each successive one was different, but showed her style in bold strokes.

After acquiring a pair of dark grey bar stools, she picked out a fat round lamp to match. That will go nicely on the end table, she decided.

She crossed the street to a little carpet and rug shop, where she picked up a large throw-rug, thick with light grey pile. She didn't want carpet— it would entirely cover the beautiful parquet floor that Joseph had installed years before, and Irene had lovingly polished. The older couple had the money to hire help, but they took pride in doing things themselves.

Satisfied with her new livingroom, Suzette paused for lunch. She found a little greasy spoon and sat down to mull over the score of *Der Rosenkavalier*. She had learned most of her role before she arrived, but the memorization was still a little shaky. She repeated the German words over and over in her head until food arrived. Glad to stop working, she hurriedly ate. She was anxious to find her bedroom suite.

Suzette decided to do the bedroom in antiques. She had seen a row of antique shops down a side street. Finding the first shop, she realized that antique shopping would take her the rest of the day. Besides all of the beautiful furniture, there were quilts, old farm equipment, clocks, old kitchen utensils, and any number of other fascinating objects to examine. Sighing, she knew she would have trouble sticking to her original goal. Suzette decided to enjoy herself a little, and stopped in front of a glass case. There she looked at the shelves heavy with jewelry, tarnished with age but still majestic. Finally she selected a heavy gold pocketwatch, the front cover engraved with a majestic five-point buck. Inside, the watch face had a small second dial on the bottom with a tiny hand that ticked off the seconds. Popping open the back, Suzette saw an inner cover that had been engraved: "50 years of faithful service." Smiling, she opened that cover to see the little cogs and springs, all gold.

"I have a friend who will love this," she told the shopkeeper, thinking of Cass and her fondness for old watches.

"That's a fine watch. Too bad it doesn't run, though. Cost a pretty penny to fix it— but maybe the gentleman knows something about watches."

Suzette just smiled. "I'll have it fixed for my friend, thanks."

Suzette returned to the apartment to find furniture stacked in crates in the livingroom. She immediately began unpacking and arranging. When the room was complete, she stopped to rest.

Irene came in and sat down on the new loveseat. "You've done wonders for this room, Susan."

"Thank you, I am rather pleased with the results." Suzette surveyed the livingroom over the brim of her teacup, her eyes resting with satisfaction on the pastel O'Keefe prints by the stairs. "The upstairs furniture won't arrive until tomorrow, but I want to stay here tonight anyway. Moving into a new place is exciting, and I want to get to know it as quickly as I can."

"I suppose you've had to get acquainted with quite a few places, haven't you dear?"

"Yes, quite a few. By the way, I may be having a guest up for the weekend."

Irene's face clouded. "Not a gentleman friend, I hope," she said, "That could be somewhat awkward."

Suzette frowned. She hadn't anticipated that problem, mostly because it hadn't occurred before. It wasn't the first time she would sin by omission. "No, my friend is a woman. Cass will probably be around fairly often. We're friends from where I live during the off seasons. . . not too far to drive."

"That must be nice for you. Maybe you can go home on the weekends sometimes."

"Yes." Suzette refused to answer Irene's tacit curiosity. "Do you attend the operas here?"

"We used to, but we've just stayed at home the past few years. We don't get out much. You must be tired after such a long day. . . I'll just clear away these cups."

The two women set their cups on the tray and Irene left. Suzette put new sheets on the sofa bed and soon was happily asleep.

The next day, as soon as Suzette's lavender princess phone had been installed, she called Fred. After
bringing him up to date on her progress, she agreed to
meet him in his office later in the day. "We never did
look over the production plans," Suzette laughed. "We
only have three days before rehearsals begin!" That
business taken care of, she called Cass.

"Hi, Cass!" she cried as soon the operator had
connected them. "The last of my furniture was delivered this morning. I thought they would never get the
bed up the stairs! But everything fit."

"That's nice." The voice on the other end was
sullen.

"What's the matter, Cass?" Suzette asked in a
softer voice.

"Nothing."

"Something's wrong, I can tell. Is it me? When you
don't talk to me, sometimes these problems get
worse."

"Nothing. . . it's just that. . . well, you didn't call me
yesterday, and I missed you. . ."

Suzette sighed. This conversation sounded familiar. "I'm sorry, darling, but I stayed in my new place,
and the phone wasn't connected. I missed you too,
dreadfully."

"Really?"

"Yes, really," Susie reassured her, "I love you very
much— don't forget that. I'll see you this weekend and
show you how much I love you. Oh, I almost forgot—
I have a surprise for you."

"You do? What is it?"

"I can't tell you that, it wouldn't be a surprise, silly
woman!"

"Well, okay. When will you be here?"

"Tonight. I'll leave here as soon as I can get away
from Fred. We're meeting this afternoon to discuss the
production."

"I might start getting jealous of Fred—you've been seeing a lot of each other," Cass teased.

"Don't be silly, he's one of us. He's not interested in women. And anyway, if he were interested in me, I would have bagged him our first year in college." Suzette almost giggled. She had chased Fred unmercifully for a year, before she realized that women were much more interesting to her than to him. "What a waste of time in the romance department." She shifted the conversation back to new furniture. "You'll laugh when you see— I bought a lesbian loveseat. It's lavender."

Cass chuckled. "How could a dyke like you be such a diva?"

After she had hung up the phone, Suzette drove her rented car down to the music building at MacAlister Community College. She was determined to practice at a piano so that she could be sure she knew her music correctly. Practicing in her little kitchen with only a pitch pipe to guide her was distinctly unsatisfying. To her dismay, the practice rooms were all locked. She marched into the musical activities office. "I," she announced, "am Suzette Etoile. I am a visiting artist for the Cosmopolitan Opera, and I would like to use one of your practice rooms. I will pay any applicable fees and deposits."

The woman at the desk was singularly unimpressed. "The key deposit is all you need, but you have to get a signed slip from the Dean. Then you have to go to the Bursar's office to pay the deposit. Bring the note and your paid deposit receipt to me, and I'll see what I can do about assigning you a room." She went back to her papers and didn't look up again.

Suzette tended to expand when she was angry. Used to having her way and intent on getting it, she swept majestically into the Dean's office. There was no secretary, so she was admitted directly in to see the

Dean. Suzette boomed out her request. The dean, a quiet, efficient woman, merely smiled. She had dealt with irate opera stars before. She really should talk to the secretary in the office downstairs.

"Of course you may use our practice rooms. I would feel privileged to know that you were singing here."

Suzette, placated, brought her voice down to a normal decibel level. "Thank you, Dean Winters. Perhaps you could tell me about your fine department over lunch someday."

"I would enjoy that." They smiled, both understanding that they would never get around to it— the offer was a formality. "Here is a master key that will let you into any practice room. I hope you find them satisfactory."

"I'm sure I will. Thank you again," Suzette called as she sailed out the door.

Arriving at the third floor, she peered in the windows of several rooms until she found an empty one. Letting herself in with her new key, she plopped her leather satchel down on the piano bench. The soundproof cubicle was just large enough to hold a baby grand piano, with room left over for a singer or instrumentalist to stand in the crook of the piano. Suzette took time to savor her last unlimited practice. Once rehearsals began, she would have to do even her warm-ups on a strict schedule.

Scales are generally dull, but for Suzette the wordless warbling had become a way to rid herself of stress. As her vocal exercises stretched higher up the scale, she released the tension of the past four days. She had sung a little every day since her arrival, just enough to keep in shape, but today she let loose. Every note strengthened her composure as well as her vocal cords. When her voice was ready to obey her slightest command, she worked diligently on her new role. The previous work she had done on the role was paying off;

when the practice session was over, she felt ready for the long staging rehearsals to come.

Suzette left the small college feeling the contentment that follows a good meal. Sated by her singing, she headed toward the C.O.C. On the way she passed a convenience store with a display of jars of soap for blowing bubbles. On impulse she entered and bought one, opened it, and blew bubbles with a childlike sense of joy all the way over to the C.O.C.

A few minutes later, Fred ushered Suzette into his office. "I don't have set models yet, just blueprints."

"That's really all I need to see right now. I just have to get some idea of the layout."

They bent to examine the carefully measured blue lines. The center line cut through the middle of the Marschallin's private entrance upstage and ran downstage to the edge of the orchestra pit. An alcove downstage left contained a big fourposter bed, where Suzette would first be seen by the audience. Across from the bed, to the audience's left, would be a large set of folding French doors about halfway upstage leading to an antechamber. On the stage right side in front of the doors there would be a dressing screen and chair. A table, a footstool, a few more chairs and a small sofa completed the furnishings. Upstage left was a large floor-length window looking out onto the drive below.

"You can see there's nothing radical in the layout. Just your basic *Rosenkavalier* set." Fred carefully rolled up the large sheet and set it aside. "Here's the second act— it seems pretty bare, but it will be breathtaking from out front."

This set had doors leading offstage on both the right and left sides. A large door placed upstage center led to an anteroom, and two huge fireplaces cut diagonally across each of the upstage corners to complete the symmetry. A few chairs were the only furniture.

"Of course the walls and fireplaces will be richly decorated for the auspicious occasion." Fred and Suzette bent to look at the Act III set.

This carefully drafted blueprint was a maze of lines. Close scrutiny was required to reveal its plan. A small curtained alcove down stage right concealed a bed. On the other side was a door leading apparently into another room. A third door upstage led into the corridor. A window looked out on nothing at all, and a fireplace filled the upstage left corner. A mirror hung over the fireplace, and every available wall held at least one wall sconce. A sideboard upstage right held a huge candelabrum, while a table for two down left held another candelabrum. The confused, maze-like quality of the drawing came from the series of dotted lines that marked various trapdoors in the floor— one under the table, one near the bed, one in front of the fireplace. This inn setting was by far the most complex of the three designs, if not the most glamorous. What it lacked in beauty was offset by its ingenuity.

Suzette leaned back, glad to rest her eyes for a moment. "Do you have all the costume sketches, too?"

"Most of them— all but yours. I sent yours back for more work." Fred leaned over and picked up one of the little metal puzzles off the credenza. When he was pleased with himself he invariably had to fidget. "I think I should tell you why I specifically wanted you to sing Octavian."

Suzette picked up the loop from the bubble soap in self defense. "I had wondered— I'm not really a mezzo-soprano."

"True, but your lower range is lovely. Not every high soprano can boast a middle and low range. And we both know you can sing the role. But the real reason is because I knew that you of all people would be willing to go along with a truly daring stroke on my part."

"Oh? What's that?"

"I want to have you costumed as what you are—a woman."

"In other words, you want to turn *Der Rosenkavalier* into a lesbian opera."

"In a word, yes."

Fred gradually unfolded the details as Suzette alternately frowned and laughed.

"What makes you so sure I'll go along with that? I may not be the same bold Susie you once knew. And besides, I have a lot to lose."

Fred was slightly annoyed. "Stop blowing bubbles. It's beginning to look like the Lawrence Welk show in here. It surprises me that you didn't name yourself Beverly."

"Careful, your age is showing. Beverly 'Bubbles' Sills hasn't been on the scene in years. Besides, I'm too old to quarrel with you."

"True." Fred sighed. "Say, why don't we order in some lunch? Pepperoni pizza okay?"

"Why not? But we'll have to do it right."

"You've got it."

"About your plan—I'll have to think about it. If I say yes, you'll still have to okay it with the other leads—especially the Marschallin and Sophie."

Fred sighed. "I know—I'm not looking forward to it. Margaret can be particularly difficult."

"I can hardly wait to meet the bitch—I mean, the woman." Suzette laughed, the last trace of seriousness vanishing.

When the pizza arrived, cold as usual, they lit some candles and dimmed the lights.

"I'll pour the Pepsi while you get the plates. Do you remember the first time we did this?"

"No. Which way shall we split it?"

"Here, like this. It was our freshman year in the lounge on our floor."

"I could've guessed that! We had lots of pizza in that lounge." Fred picked up a piece of pizza, pinching off the strings of cheese with his fingers.

"But this one was special— I can't believe you don't remember sitting there eating pizza by the light of a birthday candle stuck in a two-day-old cupcake!"

"After all, it's only been nineteen years," Fred interjected sarcastically.

Suzette continued, ignoring him. "We sat there and talked about our ambitions, our fondest daydreams. I know we did that a lot, but never as naively as the first time. I was going to have a romance that queens would envy and be a great opera singer, and you were going to be a famous concert pianist." Suzette picked up her styrofoam cup. "I guess your dream changed somewhere down the line."

"Yes and no." A tired look crept into his face. "But when you have two dreams, it's hard to know which one to pursue. You can't do both— no one has that much energy."

"I'm not entirely sure how, but I've won my first dream. I'm still working on the second." The slice of pizza hovered a moment as she thought about Cass. Coming back to the present, she glanced over at the baby grand in the corner. "Don't you play anymore, Fred?"

"Mainly this piano is for private auditions and coachings but yes, I do play some. Only when I'm alone, though."

"Perhaps you could be persuaded— for me." Suzette glided over to the floor-to-ceiling bookcases and examined the scores. "Here— let's do Suzanna's aria for old times' sake." As she pulled out *The Marriage of Figaro,* another score caught her eye. "And then I'd like to hear some Mendelssohn."

Fred obediently went to the piano and began to play. Suzette's sparkling voice soared, carrying them both back to a time and place where neither had ever been, yet each knew intimately. For a few blissful moments they existed only in the Viennese court, conducted by Mozart himself.

After the aria, Suzette was glowing with the joy she only felt after singing or making love. Contented, she sat down in Fred's big comfortable desk chair. "Now it's your turn," she told him.

Fred opened the big score. He played gingerly at first, painfully aware of Suzette. Playing Mendelssohn's "Song Without Words" had become intensely personal over the years. Soon he forgot her entirely as his whole being flowed out his fingertips onto the keyboard. When he finished, the silence echoed.

Finally, Suzette brought them both back to the present. "You've still got it— I knew you'd always be a pianist. That was beautiful," she said softly.

Fred looked embarrassed. "Don't let anyone know. Opera directors aren't supposed to be musical."

"That's a lot of garbage. Your success is largely due to the fact that you are musical— don't let the critics fool you."

"Maybe so, but let's keep it our little secret."

Chapter 3

Suzette climbed into the first taxi. Years ago, Cass would have met her at the airport, but now her arrivals were commonplace. Suzette sighed, leaning back on the cracked vinyl. Cass would at least have a warm welcome for her at home.

Suzette let her mind wander over the events of the last few days as familiar landmarks rolled past. Overall things were going well, although she hadn't decided whether or not to go along with Fred's plan. At least he had asked her, rather than telling her that it was the way the opera would be done. After all, her career could be at stake. But hadn't she been struggling for years trying to make both sides of her life come together? Opera is such a sexist world, even worse than the real one. How do I stand it? Plus, anyone who is notoriously sexist is going to be a bigger homophobe. Maybe Fred's plan is the answer to years of prayer. . . his and mine.

Suzette's thoughts turned back to Cass as the taxi swung past the mailbox proudly bearing their names. Gravel crunched under the tires as they pulled up in front of the quiet brick house. There was still no sign of Cass. Susie crossed the porch and fumbled with her keys as the taxi drove away. Gaining the front hallway, she felt a furry mass glue itself to her leg.

"Hi, Gertie, where's your momma?"

Gertie just purred, glad to have her home. Wandering into the kitchen, Susie stopped. There was Cass, her back turned, her large strong hands arranging freshly cut flowers in a vase. She turned and saw Susie standing there, businesslike in a traveling suit.

"Darling!" Instantly Cass was in Susie's arms. Red hair blended with auburn as they held each other for a long moment. Then lips met lips in a passionate kiss.

A minute later, when their breath returned, they sat down at the big butcherblock table.

"Tell me all about everything— your talks with Fred, your new place, the opera, your flight— I want to hear it all."

"But Cass, I've already told you most of that stuff." Susie laughed at her.

"I'm just so glad to have you back again that I want to hear it all again. . . or at least the details that I'm sure you left out."

"Maybe we could go out to dinner first. I haven't eaten since lunch." Remembering the pizza brought back the memory of her indecision. "I'll take you anywhere except a pizza place."

"Susie, I'm one step ahead of you. I've got dinner all ready. All we have to do is take it out of the oven and light the candles."

"You mean you actually cooked dinner for me?"

"Don't be silly. I picked up Chinese food on the way home. It's in the oven to stay warm."

"You get the chopsticks, I'll light the candles." More candles. Only this time they were were the beginning of a romantic evening, not a nostalgic trip backward into a nonexistent romance. They ate off of the paper plates provided by the restaurant. Dishes were a detested chore, and tonight anything unpleasant was to be avoided.

Susie reached across the table to take Cass' free hand. She gazed into the gold-flecked greenness of the eyes that returned her look. "Let's not talk shop tonight," she said in a low voice, "I just want to be with you. We'll have all day tomorrow to talk. . ."

"Your gear is still packed from your last move. . . all we have to do is load your car." Practical Cass always made sure the mundane necessities were accomplished before she would abandon herself. "Let's put the food away and prop our feet up for a while."

Moments later they were sitting on the sofa in their cozy living room. "It sure is good to be home," Susie sighed contentedly. She hugged Cass' red head closer to her shoulder, inhaling the fresh scent of her hair.

Cass slid her strong arm around Susie's slender waist, marveling at the way her arm fit so snugly. She never ceased to be amazed, even after five years, at how the curves and softnesses of their bodies fit together.

Holding each other quietly was enough for a while, but gradually they began to feel something was missing. At last Cass turned her freckled face invitingly up toward Susie's. Susie let her breath tickle the soft red lips offered up to her. Finally their desire moved them together into a long, sweet kiss.

They made love slowly, knowing the leisure of an evening all to themselves. The big waterbed pulsed with their bodies, magnifying each thrust a hundredfold. *Making love is an aquatic event,* floated through Susie's mind as she dove into Cass once more. Cass was beyond thought. She could only smell Susie's ocean scents and feel the waves rolling in and out as though her body was the shore.

That night they slept in disheveled happiness. Oblivious to the blankets strewn everywhere, they slept like babes, each cradled in her mother's arms.

Awakening in the crisp September dawn, Cass stretched luxuriously. Seeing her awaken, her big calico cat jumped up to sit on her chest.

"Good morning, Alice," Cass whispered, not wanting to wake up Susie—not yet. Her big hands absentmindedly stroked the cat. They were useful hands—big and strong for wielding hammers and saws, finely tuned for handling a drafting pencil, alternately gentle and powerful for making love. She had always enjoyed making things with her hands, but she claimed that sculpting Susie was the finest work those hands would ever do.

She contemplated the auburn hair spread out on the other pillow. Susie's skin was white, her freckles mere ghosts under the skin. Cass laid her hand on the pillow to compare. Her glowing bronze freckles generously overlaid on a pinkish-brown background blazed in contrast to Susie's whiteness.

Our lives are so different, yet so much alike. She traipses around the world, while I only travel in books. . . researching eras and places I've never been, so other people can go there when they see a play or an opera on my sets. Yet we're essentially doing the same thing—creating a spectacle for others, not ourselves. Helping other people leave their own lives for a few hours and enjoy themselves. If we're lucky they may even learn something from it. . . Sometimes I wish theater was still an escape for me. . . But that would be running away from life. I think Susie may still use opera as a form of escape. . .

I wish Susie was home more. . . but then I would lose a lot of my alone time. This opera should be good for us—we'll see each other more regularly—after all MacAlister is only a two hour drive. And I'll still have the time and space I need to myself.

What would I do if Susie was home all the time? She'd be fractious most of the time. . . I wouldn't get my work done. . . I'd stay home more, wanting to be with her, but I'd miss my friends, neglect my garden. . . She never has gone out with me, with other tech people, after a rehearsal or a show. But I need her. . . how can I want to be with her all the time, and at the same time hardly want her around at all?

Cass' thoughts were interrupted as the sleeping form beside her began to uncurl. Susie stretched herself in unknowing imitation of Cass.

"Good morning, lover."

Susie answered her by pulling her face down for a long kiss. Cass leaned willingly down for the kiss, but afterwards turned to get out of bed.

"Hey, where are you going? It's Saturday morning— we've got all day!"

"I know, but my bones are anxious to get moving. I'm always having to hustle to get things done, so it's hard to loll about in bed. Besides," she said, glancing at the bedside table, "it's already 9 o'clock."

"9 o'clock!" Susie moaned. "It's too early to wake up on a Saturday!"

"Then go back to sleep— I'm getting up." Cass went into the bathroom and softly shut the door.

While hot water pulsed from the showerhead onto her shoulders, Cass marveled at Susie. "When she's rehearsing I know she gets up at 5 a.m. Then when they're performing she's up at all hours and sleeps till noon. How does she adjust?" The pale blue tiles didn't answer. "That woman will never cease to amaze me."

She was drinking her second cup of coffee and watering the kitchen plants when she heard the shower go on again. She made a mental note of the time: 9:45. Not too late— lots of time for play. She dragged out her big black skillet and put some bacon on to fry.

By the time Susie arrived downstairs, Cass was sliding two fluffy omelets onto yellow and white plates.

"Coffee's ready."

"Mmm. . . cinnamon coffee!" Suzette was pleased. Cass had made her favorite. Ordinarily neither one of

29

them liked cooking, so this breakfast was a gift. Susie stood behind Cass as she worked, wrapping her arms around her waist and resting her chin on a sturdy shoulder.

"Thanks for fixing breakfast— you must love me or something."

"Of course I love you— couldn't you tell last night?"

They both smiled, remembering, enjoying the warmth of their back-to-front embrace.

Sun radiating from their faces as well as the windows lit up the little breakfast nook. Surrounded by hanging ferns, Suzette settled contentedly down at the white table. They ate in silence. For each, the other's presence said more than words.

After breakfast they went into the garden armed with plastic sacks. Suzette wasn't fond of pulling weeds, but the sooner that chore was finished, the sooner she would have Cass to herself. For the time being she had to share her with a plot full of vegetables.

Cass was in her element. She lovingly pulled up the few weeds that had grown since last week. Moving up and down the long rows, she paused to inspect an acorn squash here, an ear of corn there. The fruit of the vines were her children as much as Alice the cat was her child. She had never wanted real children, so she projected her strong motherly feelings onto other living things. Suzette admired the size and color of the various vegetables, but she never quite understood. She hadn't planted them as seeds or seedlings. She hadn't watered or tended them carefully, regarding each new leaf as a victory. She tugged impatiently at the brim of her hat.

At last the day's gardening was done. They put their gloves away in the tool shed, and Susie hung her straw hat on a nail. She slid her hand around Cass' waist, letting it rest in the curve above her hip. Cass mirrored her gesture as they walked slowly back to the house.

Sitting down to lunch, Suzette realized she'd been putting off her decision about Fred's proposal. It had been in the back of her mind all morning— a sure sign that it bothered her. Not discussing it with Cass was only making it worse. She hadn't made any progress on her dilemma alone.

"Cass, you know, don't you, that I'll be singing a pants role in *Der Rosenkavalier?*"

"Of course. You're singing Octavian, right? Don't tell me singing the role of a man makes you nervous— women have been doing it for years. It's just an operatic convention. Besides," Cass' eyes twinkled, "you shouldn't have any trouble with the love scenes."

"That's not what makes me nervous." Suzette swirled the ice around in her tea absentmindedly. "It's just that, well, Fred wants to do it a little differently."

"Go on, I'm listening," Cass coaxed. Her tone was more serious now.

Suzette decided to spit it all out at once and be done with it. "He wants me costumed as a woman."

Cass, always thinking on the technical side, said, "But won't that cause problems in the third act when Octavian is supposed to be disguised as a girl?"

Exasperated, Suzette wailed, "But you don't understand! That has nothing to do with it. This could mean my career! The whole world would know I'm a lesbian! There have always been rumors, but this would mean throwing it in their faces. Don't you see," she concluded, "this is all the critics need to get rid of me. I could be black-balled by every opera company in the country!"

"Calm down, it can't be that bad. They won't know you're a lesbian unless you tell them yourself. Otherwise the blame will fall on the director. Fred will have to take all the flack."

"I know," Suzette admitted, considerably calmer. "But. . ."

"Something's still bothering you. What is it, Susie?" Cass asked gently, reaching out to stroke her lover's hair. "Please trust me."

"I'm just not nearly as adventurous as I used to be, but. . ." She sighed and pushed aside her plate, laying her head on her arms. Her next words were muffled. "I'm tired of lying."

Cass slid a reassuring arm across her shoulders.

"I understand, love. I'm tired of lying, too. The people I work with wouldn't care. I'm sure a lot of them know anyway. But I've always kept quiet for your sake." Cass knew she was lucky—most people suspected women techies of being dykes anyway. Her job wouldn't be in danger.

"I hate myself," Suzette burst out. "All I am is a lie. I lied to Joseph and Irene. . . they wanted to ban men from my apartment, thinking they were banning sex. I just let them believe it. And that's only the most recent incident. I've been lying for years. My whole career is based on a lie, because I'm a coward." Suzette sobbed into the tablecloth until Cass took her and held her close.

"It's okay, it's okay," she crooned. "We'll figure something out."

Later when Susie had calmed down, Cass offered her suggestions. "The way I see it, you have three choices. Obviously you could refuse to do it, which would be the most reliable method of staying 'safe.' Or you could go along with it, and let Fred take the blame. You'd have to do a lot of fancy lying, maybe find a boyfriend somewhere, and I'd stay out of the way for a while. I wouldn't like it, sweetie, but I'd do it for you— and for us. The third option is to come out publicly. You could probably wait till the opera's over if you want. If you were to come out publicly, you don't know what would happen. No one's done it before, at least not before their career was over."

"I know— that's what scares me."

"Wait— I'm not finished. Several things could happen. We've got to look at this rationally or we'll both go crazy." Cass paused a moment to put her thoughts in order. "You might be black-balled in America, as you say, but there are other countries where it wouldn't matter as much— you could probably still sing. Or you could drop out of sight for a while, change your name, start fresh somewhere else."

"Start over. . . you must be kidding."

"It's entirely up to you— if you thought it was necessary. I'm just trying to explore the possibilities. There's always the chance that nothing would happen. After all, your average Jane Doe thinks that all theater people, musicians in particular, are gay anyway. If the men can get away with it, why can't you? One good thing, at least, would come from coming out. You wouldn't have to lie anymore."

"That's the only positive aspect... no more lying..."

They pondered the possibilities for a moment. Cass was the first to break the silence.

"Susie. . ." her voice was gentle. "Even if you were to go along with it, I don't see how Fred could pull it off."

"You sound like you're trying to talk me out of it."

"Not necessarily. I'm trying to be realistic— besides, you're doing a good enough job of talking yourself out of it. It's just that Fred would have to rewrite the whole opera. There are too many things that won't work the way it's written. The biggest problem would be the scenes where Octavian is disguised as 'Mariandl,' the bastard serving girl. And the sword fight with Baron Ochs. . ."

"I know," interrupted Suzette, "But Fred has the boy-girl switch worked out to be an upper-class woman to servant girl switch. And the sword fight—she grabs a big curved blade from one of the Hussars who serves her as a footman."

"It sounds like a lame excuse for a crazy re-adaptation of the opera, if you ask me. There are a lot of little things, too; little jokes, asides. . ." Cass' brow furrowed. She didn't think it would work.

"It's true it would be hard to do, but if he's worked it out already. . ." Suzette paused. "I think I also need to consider the integrity of the work. I've always felt that a piece should be done as the composer wrote it. What would Richard Strauss think of all this?"

"That is something to consider. Your integrity as an artist may be at stake here, more than your sexuality and popularity."

"After all, the work is already sexually ambiguous. The audience watches Octavian as boy, even though intellectually they know she's a woman. They simply blind themselves to the fact." Suzette sighed. "Thanks for helping me sort it out, Cass. I'll have to say no."

Once the decision was made, the subject was closed. Suzette plugged the 1932 movie *Grand Hotel* into the VCR, and the women spent half an hour admiring Joan Crawford and Greta Garbo.

"Greta looks so much better in still shots," Suzette sighed. She held up her remote control device and punched "off." "Let's get out of here."

"How about a ride?"

"Marvelous! I haven't been on horseback in ages."

The local stables weren't far, but the brisk walk lifted their spirits. The brief ride in the late afternoon sun left both of them refreshed, filled with the sights and smells of early autumn. The exercise gave them a hearty appetite. After indulging in a big dinner, they were both ready to turn in.

The next morning, Suzette was the first to rise. She was anxious to get her car packed and get back to

MacAlister. There was no need to arrive early, but she was excited about the upcoming rehearsal. After a few weeks the opera would be wearing on her nerves, she knew, but the first day was always special.

"Damn."

"What's the matter, love?" Cass was roused out of sleep by the bathroom door slamming open.

"I'm bleeding. Just what I need! Tomorrow's the first sing-through and I'm not going to be at my best." Suzette's superstitions were acting up again. "A bad first rehearsal bodes ill for the production."

"If that were true, all shows would be doomed." Cass rolled over. She figured she had fifteen more minutes to sleep.

Suzette stomped downstairs. Once she reached the kitchen, however, she became preoccupied with measuring out the coffee. After drinking her first cup, she felt much better.

Later, after she and Cass had eaten a quick break-fast, Suzette headed for the garage. Several boxes and suitcases were waiting there to be loaded into her old red Honda stationwagon. She carefully placed her stereo into the tiny back seat, tossing the suitcases and hanging bags full of clothing into the back.

"Did you get it all loaded?" Cass called from the garden.

"All set. Now I can relax a few more hours."

Around 4:00 p.m. Suzette and Cass kissed good-bye. It wasn't a sad parting. They were each ready to get on with their work in the coming week. Life, they decided, isn't too bad when you're a hundred miles apart.

Chapter 4

Unpacking her clothes and hanging them in the big wardrobe, Suzette thought about the upcoming rehearsal. She never slept well before a new opera began. She had made a habit of not sleeping well before important events. For twelve years of public school and seven years of college she had had the same problem before the first day of each semester. It never became a problem, though, because her adrenaline always carried her through the crucial day.

She knew she should call Fred to explain why she couldn't go along with his crazy plan, but she put it off until morning. "Tomorrow is soon enough," she told Gertie, who was sniffing cautiously around the strange room. "I know I'm doing the right thing, but still, I wish there was a way to bring the two halves of my life together. You'd think that by having a lover in the theater business it would be easier, but it isn't. It just gives us something to talk about, something in common." She went downstairs to assemble her stereo in the living room, the grey furry form gliding silently down behind her. She settled into the couch and propped her feet up on the coffee table. Suzette realized that her dual lives hadn't bothered her in a long time. At least, not this much. The problem had always stayed just beneath the surface of her mind.

She was aware of it only as an annoying itch. But the whole idea of coming out publicly by turning *Der Rosenkavalier* into a lesbian opera had brought the duality to the surface again. Try as she might, she couldn't submerge it again, not as completely as it had been.

She sighed, and set to work wiring her stereo components together. At least doing something would help pass the time until morning and keep her from dwelling on the subject. After she finished, she went to bed. She wanted to attempt to sleep, anyway.

She must have slept better than expected, for she awoke to bright sunshine. The early morning sun fell in a window pane pattern across the quilt, bathing a contented Gertie in its warmth.

"Time to get up, you lazy cat," she told her.

Suzette started the coffee, then headed into the shower. Singing in the shower was part of her morning routine, but not an average shower concert— she used the opportunity to warm up each morning. Gertie would run and hide when Suzette sang; it hurt her sensitive ears.

The coffee had been ready for some time when she climbed out of the shower. Pouring a cup, she grimaced. She preferred her coffee white with sugar, but she always drank it black when she had to sing. The cream and sugar created too much nasty slime in her throat. She knew she shouldn't drink it at all before singing because the caffeine dried her out, but the most she was willing to do was compromise. She'd drink lots of water later to make up for it.

Before getting dressed she did a few stretching exercises. She knew that Fred had always insisted on stretches before staging rehearsals, so she went easy on her own exercises. Then she selected an olive green sweater to set off her hair. Appearances were important at the first rehearsal if the rest of the cast was going to respect her. The chorus was particularly important to impress. They were most easily influenced by an honest, hard-working artist. Prima donna behavior only caused them to grumble. They would become sluggish, not responding to directions well. She knew that they would give Fred, as well as herself, a hard time if she and the other leads were not on their mettle today.

She finished dressing and went downstairs. Sitting on the floor in front of the couch, she set a small alarm clock on the coffee table. She wanted to be sure that she meditated long enough, without being late. Gertie curled up on the sofa behind Suzette to stare out of her big yellow eyes. Finally bored, the cat disappeared up the stairs to continue her explorations.

A tiny beeping sound roused Suzette out of her meditations, and she gathered up everything she needed for the day. She fed the cat and was gone.

Suzette arrived about fifteen minutes early. Fred was there, along with a few other singers.

"Good morning, Fred. What's on the schedule today?"

"Well, after we sing through the whole opera I'd like to start at the beginning. We'll probably only get to stage the scene between you and the Marschallin up to the entrance of the Baron, so I'll let everyone else go early."

More of the cast filed in, until almost everyone was present. Gregory Loft, who was singing the role of Baron Ochs, arrived right on the half hour. Finally everyone had found their places except Margaret Byrd. The cast shuffled uneasily as they waited. Margaret, as the Marschallin, opened the opera, so she knew they couldn't begin without her.

"Damn her, she's got to make an entrance," Suzette whispered through clenched teeth to the young woman seated next to her. And make an entrance she did. Margaret came sweeping in at 8:40—ten minutes after the rehearsal was scheduled to begin. She had coal-black hair with just a few wisps of grey, a sharp contrast to her ivory white skin. She wore a red silk dress with tiny grey marks scattered through it like slashes of rain. The fullness of the bodice billowed as she walked, giving glimpses of her ample cleavage to anyone who cared to look. Her shoulder-length hair streaming behind her like a banner, she marched grandly to the front of the stage and took her place with assurance in the center of the front row. Her black eyes snapped defiantly, daring Fred to cross her, even as her full red lips smiled graciously at him.

"Now that we're all here," Fred announced, "I'd like to welcome you to our all-new production of *Der Rosenkavalier* here at the Cosmopolitan Opera. I'd like to present to you our conductor, Christophe Kleinemann. For those of you who also don't know our leads, I'll introduce them. Margaret Byrd will be the Marschallin, or, as Octavian so fondly calls her, 'Bichette.'"

Margaret stood and gave a curt nod to the chorus.

"Our Count Octavian Maria Ehrenreich Bonaventura Fernand Hyacinth Rofrano is Suzette Etoile." Fred obviously enjoyed his mastery of the name, much as Sophie does in the second act.

Suzette rose and smiled a "hello" to the cast. Each of the others also rose briefly as their names were announced.

"Baron Ochs von Lerchenau will be Gregory Loft." A distinguished, though heavy set and slightly balding man rose. He smiled warmly at Fred, his clear blue eyes sparkling mischeviously. Suzette couldn't help smiling as well. Greg's good humor was so infectious, Suzette almost missed the next few introductions. "Daniel Forsythe is singing Herr Faninal, Sophie's father. Our Sophie Faninal is Jennifer Doyle."

The slender young woman next to Suzette rose. Suzette looked at Jennifer thoughtfully, appraising the fine brown hair swept back from her brow, exposing her warm brown eyes. Though not tall, Jennifer held herself proudly. Only a hint of timidity was visible to Suzette's experienced eye. Suzette decided that the young woman would make an excellent Sophie, provided she could sing. Presumably she could. Jennifer was a recent "discovery" by the C.O.C. Young singers just didn't get in unless they were of exceptional merit. Suzette knew that her youth, her pretty face and petite figure had helped her to get the role of Sophie. But then, Sophie was supposed to be fifteen. The role wasn't quite as convincing when sung by a forty-year-old soprano with a waist that would support a Brunnhilde voice. Suzette knew that Jennifer's looks would have helped her get the role anywhere, but at least here it was *strictly* a matter of type casting. She was one of the few people who would never suspect Fred of sleeping with his young starlets.

She hadn't heard the rest of the roll call, since she had been busy looking around at the rest of the cast—particularly Jennifer. She was roused from her musings by the beginning of the overture on the piano. She knew that the overture didn't end, but rather, went directly into the first lines of singing. She stood to prepare herself. Margaret, the only other singer involved in the opening scene, didn't bother to rise until just before her musical entrance. They both sang well, and they could hear murmurs of approval from behind them.

Fred was making a point of not stopping the sing-through unless absolutely necessary. The idea behind the sing-through was to give the whole cast an idea of what the opera was supposed to sound like, and to give everyone a sense of continuity. No one would hear it in its entirety again until they had another sing-through. The second would be with orchestra rather than piano, and wouldn't take place until a week and a half before the opera opened.

At the end of Act I, Maestro Kleinemann gave everyone a break. Suzette took the opportunity to greet Jennifer Doyle.

"Hello, I'm Suzette. Have you sung with the C.O.C. before?"

"No, you could call this my debut. I got lucky."

"This is my debut here, too, but I worked for it." Suzette laughed. "I'm just teasing— anyone who gets here at your age has worked at it somewhere. Would you like to have dinner?"

"Cast to stage, please. Break's over!" The stage manager's voice broke in over the loudspeaker.

"Sure," Jennifer said as she and Suzette made their way back to the stage.

Arriving back at their seats, Suzette realized that her abdomen was in pain. "Damn," she thought, "I forgot to go to the bathroom and change my diapers." She hadn't noticed the mild cramps while she was singing— nor while she had been distracted by Jennifer. She had some time before her first entrance, so she made her way through the wings to a restroom.

"Hello, Miss Byrd."

Margaret eyed her in the mirror as she carefully penciled in a smudged eyebrow. "It's Mrs. Byrd, but call me Mahgaret, dahling."

Suzette hurried past into the first stall. She was slightly uneasy. Something about that woman made her nervous. The look Margaret had given her in the mirror seemed to size her up fairly accurately. "I'd better keep my eye on her," Suzette decided. "She could be dangerous." When she stepped out to wash her hands, Margaret was gone.

The second act went fairly smoothly. Everyone was doing their best to make their entrances, stay in tempo, and just generally stay on top of things. It was a good cast. They were already committed to working with each other, rather than against each other.

Concentration waned a bit during the third act, but that was to be expected. All told, it was an excellent first reading of the opera. Suzette and Fred were in high spirits as they went off to have lunch.

"I'm pleased that even the people with smaller roles have worked so hard on their music," Suzette said between bites of sandwich.

"And I'm pleased that Margaret knew hers so well—she's not often this well prepared. She hasn't sung this role in a long time." Fred sipped his vending-machine soda.

"I was quite impressed with our Sophie—what's her name again?"

"You know that as well as I do—I noticed your interest." Fred grinned slyly.

"Oh, you did, did you?" Suzette stared him down. "I assure you that my interest was purely vocal."

"Yes, you can be rather vocal at times."

Suzette laughed and poked him in the ribs. "Go away—your puns are dreadful. By the way, I'm afraid I've got to turn down your plan. I feel that it might jeopardize the integrity of the opera, because of all the major changes that would have to take place in order for it to work. I think if you want to do an opera of that sort, you should commission one to be written. Let me know if you do!"

Suzette was surprised to see relief instead of disappointment register on Fred's face. "I was hoping you'd say that—I let my desire to do it run away with my common sense. I wasn't entirely pleased with my ideas for the re-write. Besides, it was too risky for my career, but I couldn't resist trying!"

They quickly finished the rest of their lunch and disposed of the pile of sticky plastic wrappers.

After lunch they began the real rehearsing. Fred staged the love scene between the Marschallin and Octavian. Both singers behaved with professional decorum, and the staging went quickly.

Later Suzette reviewed the day with pleasure as she drove home to change. Altogether a good day, she decided. A good omen for the production.

Dinner with Jennifer was singularly uneventful. They had talked only on the usual mundane topics... where they had gone to school, what roles they had sung, their hopes for this opera. Suzette felt unreasoning relief. It didn't seem kosher to become attracted to someone she barely knew, after a lovely weekend with her lover of five years. Suzette dismissed the thought. She must just be glad to have started rehearsals, after all the tense build-up of last week.

Tuesday and Wednesday sped past in a flurry of rehearsals and coachings. Suzette was entirely caught up in her work. By Thursday, though, she had begun to settle down. After an intense coaching, the last for the day, she felt the need for more companionship than Gertie alone could provide. Climbing into her battered little car she headed out to Fred's.

Suzette saw Fred before she could see the house. He was raking the leaves along the picket fence that enclosed the garden.

"Surely you don't intend to rake the whole orchard?" she called. She hopped out of her car and walked up to him as he stopped to wave.

"No, of course not," he replied as she drew near. "I just need a few layers of leaves for my compost pile." He stripped off worn leather work gloves. "You look like you need a drink. Let's walk up to the house."

"I could use a friendly cup of cocoa. Heavy on the friendly, please."

"What's the matter?" Fred asked as they strolled around the curve in the driveway.

"Nothing serious, I'm just lonely. Cass will be up tomorrow, but I need a little human companionship today."

"I know how that is— I often get lonely out here."

"Don't you have plenty of 'overnight guests,' or at least friends you can ask over?"

"Not really. I have very few friends. I have to keep my distance from most of my colleagues. Either out of respect for them, their respect for me, or nasty competitive attitudes. Besides, I get tired of talking shop all the time."

"So what would you rather talk about? What are your other interests these days?"

"Not much— just gardening and sex. Most people don't talk gardening and won't talk sex. Besides, those are both activities, not topics."

"Between you and me, however, they must remain topics. I garden at home just to be with Cass but that's as far as I go with it, and, well, the other is self-explanatory." They both chuckled.

Reaching the house, they decided to enjoy the last rays of sun. Suzette sat on the porch while Fred went in for the hot chocolate. The sky to her left was just beginning to deepen into shades of red, mingling with blues and greens. The mysteries of the color spectrum slowly unfolded as the primaries blended into spectacular hues of purple and orange. Suzette and Fred sipped their drinks in silence, warming their hands on the big mugs as they watched.

Finally Fred broke the silence. "So what do you need?"

"What do you mean?"

"I know you came out here for some reason. . . but if you don't want to tell me, that's fine."

Suzette smiled into the steam still rising from her cup, warming her face. "I'm not sure why, Fred, except that you're the only friend I have here. Even though we haven't seen each other in ten years." She paused, trying to puzzle out her own motivations. "Maybe it's partly because of my inner turmoil." She stressed the words with a comical accent, making the ludicrous term even more absurd. She was joking, but in a way it was true. Seeming to change the subject, she said, "I've been watching Jennifer Doyle. She's quite professional for such a young singer."

"Careful, Susie, you're taken. Don't mess up a good thing for a backstage romance."

"Honestly, what makes you think I'm heading for such a thing? I haven't had a backstage fling for over five years—not since pre-Cass days—and I'm not likely to start again now."

Suzette was troubled. *Could Fred be right? A crush? And at my age!*

"If you say so." Fred shrugged off the subject. "So what do you think of Princess Margaret?"

"A dangerous character. I've noticed how she flirts with you—and every male in the cast. Does she really try to get you into bed?"

"Yes, really. And I've noticed her interest in you."

"You can't be serious."

"I am serious, and I don't mean a professional interest, either. She's acting too well in that love scene with you—it's only the first week of rehearsals. She doesn't usually get into character until just before the production opens. And besides that, she believes that beautiful singing is the most important part of an opera. She says that as an excuse for her bad acting."

Suzette brushed the subject off as preposterous.

"Believe what you wish, Susie, but just remember what I've told you. And be careful."

They spent the rest of the evening reminiscing. Laughter allowed Suzette to return home with a light heart. Backstage romances were a myth, and tomorrow night she would be with Cass.

Chapter 5

Suzette was blissfully ignorant of everyone on Friday.

She was busy thinking of Cass. The anticipation of the coming evening prevented her from monitoring Margaret or admiring Jennifer. In a coaching with Dr. Kleinemann, the maestro had to stop and call her attention to the music.

"You make mistakes today! At the top of the page you sing wrong notes. This is not like you, Suzette— yesterday you knew this! Start again, same place. And this time think!"

His exasperation at the day's sloppy work forced her to concentrate. Thanks to the sheer force of her will, she made it through the rest of the coaching. Making herself concentrate, work, learn, she expended twice as much energy as she would use on a day when her whole mind was on the rehearsal.

Released at last, she hurried home to tidy up before Cass arrived. They had not yet begun weekend rehearsals, so tomorrow was free. They had been invited out to Fred's. . . Susie knew that Fred and Cass were anxious to meet each other. After all, she met Cass five years after she had lost touch with Fred, and she spoke about each to the other quite frequently. Still, she was anxious for them to like each other.

Just as she put dinner in the oven, there was a knock on the door. She unbolted it and flung it wide.

"Cass! I'm so glad to see you!" A few minutes later she murmured into the curve of her neck, "I've missed you so— I could hardly sing today for thinking of you." She pulled away and held her at arms' length. "The maestro even had to call me down for mistakes!" She laughed and pulled her close again.

"Funny," Cass said, "Thoughts of me used to make you sing better."

"It depends on what my thoughts are. If I'm just remembering how sweet and gorgeous you are, or how kind you are to me, I sing my best. My voice just won't quit. But when I remember how you tease me, how you run your hands and body and tongue all. . ."

Her words were stopped by Cass' mouth. After the searing kiss had ended, Cass finished for her. "I know. You can't sing because those wonderful naughty thoughts take your breath away. Heaven knows you can't sing without breath!" She laughed. "So give me the grand tour!"

Suzette obliged, and Cass made all the appropriate noises of approval. She was particularly approving when they reached the kitchen on the second floor.

"Mmm. . . smells delicious," she said into the hot mouth of the oven. "It's awfully sweet of you to make dinner." The two-hour drive had made her hungry.

"The chicken has to bake for 45 minutes. . . let me show you the rest."

They went upstairs. Cass gasped at the breathtaking lightness of the room. When she first reached the top of the stairs, the windows gave her the illusion of being out in the open, suspended in mid-air. A split second later she returned to earth, but not before noticing the wonderful old grandmother oak tree.

"This room is magnificent," she stated before she had actually seen the room itself. While she was exploring the interior of the bedroom, Suzette opened the tall wardrobe and removed a red velvet box.

"I was going to give this to you last weekend, but I forgot. It's your surprise."

Cass opened the jewelry case. There lay the gold watch, ticking the seconds into the red velvet. Cass just looked at Susie, delight shining in her eyes. She explored the watch more carefully than she had explored the apartment. She laughed at the inscription before opening the inner back case. The works mesmerized her, the gold spring moving back and forth with perfect precision. The finger-like teeth of the cogs meshed together and parted again like lovers or lives. A mechanical wonder— fascinating her.

When her horizon expanded again to include the room, she threw her arms around Susie's neck like a little kid. She couldn't find words, but Susie read her thanks in her excitement. Cass gave her a quick kiss. Thinking better of it, she kissed her again, only this time slowly. The kiss grew longer until Susie's knees began to give way. She bent them down to the bed, but sitting was awkward. Lying down seemed the most natural and convenient solution. Once the two women had stretched out, they forgot why they had been standing. Hands and lips began to roam of their own accord.

Lost in the scents and sounds of each other's bodies, their surroundings became irrelevant. Even time lay forgotten, placed gently on the bedside table with the gold watch.

Abruptly other noises pierced their senses. A high, nasal buzzing made them jump to their feet.

"What in heaven's name. . ."

"It's the smoke alarm. . ." Suzette hit the floor running. "My chicken!"

Suzette flipped off the oven and pulled out a pan full of smoking charcoal, then pulled a chair under the smoke alarm. By this time Cass reached the kitchen and opened the window.

Suzette banged on the smoke alarm. "The damn thing won't shut off," she yelled at Cass. "There's no switch." The smoke slowly began to clear. Cass went back upstairs to open the big windows while Suzette tried to disembowel the alarm. At last, for no apparent reason, the alarm stopped. Suzette sank to the chair in relief.

"I think it knew its days were numbered," she said, waving at the smoke alarm.

Cass pulled a chair up beside her. "I thought I was going to have a heart attack when that thing went off..."

"That's funny, I thought you were going to have an orgasm." Susie grinned slyly.

The red rising in Cass' face clashed with her carroty hair. "So what are we going to do about dinner?" she asked abruptly, changing the subject. "I'm starved."

Suzette was about to reply when they heard a knock on the door. "Saved by the bell— so to speak." She fastened her blouse, smoothed out her skirt and went downstairs.

Predictably, it was Irene at the door. "I heard the noise— are you all right?"

"Yes, we're fine. I burned our dinner, that's all." By this time Cass had dressed and joined them. "Allow me to introduce my friend, Cassandra Kelley. Cass, this is Irene Thayer."

"I'm so pleased to meet you, dear. I've heard all about you."

That's what you think, Cass thought. Aloud she said, "I've heard a lot about you, too, Mrs. Thayer."

"Please call me Irene. We're all friends here."

If you only knew. "Thank you— Irene."

The three women sat down in the living room, making small talk. Cass was careful to keep her knees together. Suzette clasped her hands tightly in her lap, afraid they might stray over to Cass' thigh without consulting her first. After an awkward pause Suzette realized they were waiting for her to say something.

"I'm sorry, what did you say?"

"Irene has asked us over for dinner, since ours is ruined." Cass smiled at Susie's momentary bewilderment. She knew what she had been thinking about. "Susie, why didn't you tell me that Irene raises orchids?"

"Hmm? Oh, you didn't ask. . ." her brain was still slightly fogged with desire, and she was trying to think about the first question. She didn't feel hungry. The uppermost thought in her mind was to get Cass alone again. "Irene, I think we can scrounge up something for dinner. I appreciate. . ."

Cass interrupted. "But I would love to have dinner with Irene and Joseph. I want to find out more about their hothouse garden."

Suzette yielded. She knew that the pleasure she had anticipated was only postponed, not cancelled.

Dinner was a fugue of polite manners and side-stepped questions woven into a detailed conversation on gardening. Suzette relaxed and enjoyed Irene's good home cooking. She knew it would be useless to drag Cass away early. If she did, Cass would be sullen, souring the evening. Cass was in her element. She loved talking about gardening almost as much as planting and pulling weeds. Suzette sighed. It seemed that everyone was into gardening except her.

At last the dinner wound to a close. They bid the Thayers good night and went back through the breezeway to Suzette's apartment.

"Thanks for going to dinner with them— I know you wanted to stay home."

"That's all right. I wanted you to have a good time..." Suzette yawned. Sitting down on the edge of the bed, she was suddenly overcome by a wave of sleepiness. Brushing it aside, she pulled Cass to her. She was determined to have Cass to herself for a while. Sleep was not going to stop her.

"Now, where were we when we were so rudely interrupted?" Suzette asked, then answered herself by kissing Cass tenderly.

Cass returned her kiss warmly. They began to undress each other slowly, patiently. But when their blouses and skirts had hit the floor, they could no longer be patient. They made quick work of the remaining clothing, tossing garments left and right with abandon. As the last pair of panties ridiculously festooned a lampshade, they sank in unison to the bed. The velvet feel of skin on skin was intoxicating. Arms and legs, hands and lips intermingled until neither woman could identify her own. The dry velvet melted into wet velvet until their bodies trembled. The leaves outside shook an empathetic accompaniment as the deep chords swelled within them. The harmonies crescendoed into a plagal cadence, the amen of their hymn to life. The postlude brought warm feelings of comfort. Suzette, exhausted from the taxing day, fell asleep with her fingers still gloved in Cass' wetness. Cass lay enjoying the comfort of Susie's still fingers, her deep, untroubled breathing. She was lulled into sleep by the ticking of the watch on the bedside table.

The next evening they drove out to Fred's. Cass chastised Suzette when she saw the garden and orchard. "You want to keep all these people to yourself, don't you. You didn't tell me all your friends here were gardeners! First Irene, now Fred. I think I'm going to enjoy coming up here on weekends."

"I should hope so— even without people to talk dirt with. After all, I'm here— I think I could keep you occupied." The naughty twinkle in her eye conveyed exactly what she meant.

"I'm sure you could," Cass teased back, "but sometimes it feels good to get out of bed. I know that's hard for you to comprehend."

Fred was waiting on the porch. "Greetings!"

"Hi, Fred! This is my lover, Cass Kelley." It felt so good to say that— to call Cass her lover out loud, to another human being. "Cass, this is my old friend, Fred Carlsen."

"I've heard so much about you."

"Same here." This time the little formalities had a ring of truth. Fred, winking at Cass, ushered them both inside. "So how do you like living with a diva?"

"It's a challenge," Cass said, laughing at Suzette, "but fun. I wouldn't trade the unpredictability of it for anything."

The two women settled into the sofa as Fred went off to get a round of sodas. Cass already found the house comfortable. It had a cozy, inviting air. She could see why anyone would feel at home— the sofa was close to the big stone fireplace, a dark persian rug creating the sense of an intimate space. Yet behind the sofa were plush chairs and a few small tables arranged in other small groupings— perfect for the casual cocktail party.

"Suzette tells me that all the cast parties are held out here. I can see why," Cass complimented Fred as he returned from the kitchen.

"The only drawback is that I get kitchen duty— I have to repair the damage done by the caterers." Fred smiled. "A small price to pay for a big bash."

Suzette let them chat uninterrupted. She just sat back and watched pieces of her scattered life come together. How strange, to see two of her most intimate friends meet. There was a rightness about it. It seemed especially strange, not that they were meeting, but that they had never met before. They had met, though, in a way. They had both been completely absorbed by

Suzette. Cass felt this, too. Talking to Fred was a lot like talking to Susie— he seemed, at first, her male counterpart. Of course, part of the ease they found in speaking with each other was due to their more concrete second-hand knowledge, willingly offered in Suzette's conversations. She told Cass about everyone she had ever known, but only a select few, like Fred, had been told at length about Cass. Seeing Fred and Cass amiably talking filled Suzette with a sense of pride, accomplishment. But the accomplishment was dimmed by the fact that nothing really new had been done.

Dinner was seasoned with the comfortable conversation of old friends. As Susie and Cass were leaving, Cass reached out impulsively and gave Fred a big hug. Fred, caught by surprise, returned it warmly.

Later, lying in bed, Suzette queried Cass on the evening. She was anxious for her two friends to get along. They had seemed fine, but she was a little insecure when something was important to her.

"So what do you think of Fred?" she asked, trying not to sound concerned.

"He's very nice— I know that 'nice' is a tame word, but it seems to fit."

"How profound. Can't you be more specific?"

"Well, I'll try, since it seems to matter so much." Susie blushed as Cass continued. "He seems insecure, especially for someone who's so well established. Oh, I know," she hurried as Suzette tried to object. "It's subtle. . . under the surface. But I could see it tonight. I have a feeling that he probably hides it better in public. But I really do like him," she assured Susie.

Susie let the subject drop. Cass had obviously been telling the truth. She wasn't exactly sure what kind of reaction, what affirmation she had wanted. She kissed Cass good night and turned out the lamp. Rolling over, she felt the S-curve of Cass folding onto her back. Her warmth radiated well-being that had been missing during Susie's week. She sighed happily, snuggled into the warmth, and sank into sleep.

Sunlight peeked timidly through the east window the next morning, gradually growing bolder until Suzette could no longer sleep. Waking up first on a weekend morning was unusual, so she decided to enjoy it. Turning away from the sun, she admired the finer features of the face on the pillow beside her. The strong line of jaw softened a little in sleep. Susie was fiercely proud of the aggressiveness it wore during the day, but she loved the vulnerable beauty of it when Cass wasn't on her guard. Her long fire-red hair was always bound into a pony-tail when Cass was working, hanging in one long stream down to the small of her back. Now it was loose, spreading suggestively across her shoulder and breast, allowing just the nipple to peek through its silky strands. Susie couldn't resist touching that nipple, teasing it with a damp finger. Cass flung her arm upward in unaimed defense just before she awoke.

"Woman, what do you think you're doing?" Cass was a little disgruntled at her wake-up call.

"Nothing. . . I just couldn't resist your dazzling beauty, that's all." Suzette leaned over and kissed her softly, then more urgently. Cass brushed her off and rolled over. "What's wrong? I just wanted to kiss you."

"That's not true— you want more than just a kiss, I can tell from the way you kissed me. I don't feel like making love right now."

"That's not what I meant at all," Suzette lied, on the defensive now. "I really just wanted a kiss. I wouldn't mind making love now, though. I won't see you again for a whole week."

"I know, but there's more to life than sex and work." Cass rolled back over to look Susie in the eye. "Isn't there?"

Taken slightly aback, Suzette replied, "Of course there is, darling. You're important to me as a person, not just a sex object. I just. . ."

"Never mind. What would you like for breakfast?" Cass brushed off the subject just as she had brushed Susie off moments earlier. She gave Susie a quick little peck on the cheek and rolled out of bed. "First dibs on the shower."

Breakfast was a silent affair. The early morning incident hung ominously over their heads. Later, as Cass was packing to leave, the storm broke.

The argument was a theme with variations, practiced occasionally during the course of their relationship. They hurled the same half-truths and false accusations back and forth, the words meaningless objects. The act of throwing words had a physical force, forming a release for pent up anger. Little frustrations with their jobs, with each other, with their self-inflicted closets, with the world at large had collected in them until it overflowed. Eventually their words crashed into a climax, quickly subsiding. The words spent, their tears of rage flowed smoothly into tears of remorse. The transition to mutual consoling passed unnoticed. They simply realized that their anger belonged, for the most part, elsewhere.

When the women had dried each other's tears, they felt relief slowly replenish their spirits.

"At least we cleared the air," Susie sniffled.

Cass smiled, the sun after a shower. "We sure did, with a vengeance."

They held each other quietly for a while, recovering themselves and clinging to their last few moments together. The bond between the two women hadn't ripped apart in the explosion, but had strengthened instead.

It was hard for Cass to leave Susie. She was feeling protective of Susie's newly raw nerves. Likewise, Susie wanted to take care of Cass, to cradle her and make the world go away. They stroked each other's tear-streaked faces, their kisses lingering. Both were reluctant to end the weekend just when they felt so close.

"I'll come up again next weekend." Cass reassured Susie with a kiss.

She left in a cloud of exhaust. Susie plugged an old Crawford movie into her VCR to pass the evening. She stared at the graceful images on the screen, biding her time until she could sleep. She found herself impatient for Monday morning and the return of her weekday world.

Chapter 6

Monday's work forced Suzette to put Cass out of her mind, as predicted. Fred made them run through the staging again and again. He obviously wasn't pleased, but the cast was working hard. Act III was just difficult to coordinate. Octavian and company are playing tricks on Baron Ochs. The appearances of the ghouls and ghosts have to be timed just right or the scene doesn't work. Finally Fred dismissed them for lunch. Suzette waylaid him on the way to the cafeteria.

"You're in a tizzy today. You know the only way to handle a difficult rehearsal is to keep your cool."

"I usually do."

"Well today you didn't. What's really wrong?" Suzette knew he was generally good at keeping up a professional front.

"I think I'm getting my period."

Suzette hissed in his ear, "You old queen." They chuckled, but Suzette was worried. Fred evidently didn't want to discuss it in public.

Fred watched himself the rest of the day. He didn't want to take his personal problems out on the cast. The afternoon went quickly. Everyone felt Fred's mood swing upward. Most of the cast didn't realize the reason, but somehow the staging seemed easier. The innkeeper and waiters flew about with delightful agility. Ghosts made their cues and the Baron turned left or right with perfect timing to discover them. Octavian flirted exceptionally well.

Suzette loved this scene. Her character, Octavian, was masquerading as a serving girl, Mariandel. Suzette liked being a woman playing a boy who was disguised as girl. The ambiguity amused her greatly.

When they stopped for a break, Gregory Loft pulled Suzette off to one side and complimented her. "Nice work," Greg said, then shifted into his Baron Ochs voice. "I'd say you were really a girl, if I didn't know better!"

They both laughed, then headed for the coffee machines.

Once they were comfortably settled with their steaming cups, Greg leaned close to Suzette. "I'm worried about Fred. He wasn't himself this morning."

"Who was he?" Suzette quipped, then changed her tone. "Sorry. Bad joke. I've been worried about him today, too. He seemed better this afternoon, but I suspect he was putting on an act for the cast's benefit."

"I'm sure of it. That's why I wanted to talk to you— I know you're good friends. Would you talk to him?"

"I was planning to call him tonight, but you could talk to him instead, if you'd rather."

"No, I— I can't. Won't you, for Fred's sake? He was quite disturbed."

"Of course. Besides, I was going to anyway." With that, the topic was dropped, and Suzette and Greg chatted about opera until time for the rehearsal to reconvene.

The rest of the rehearsal continued to go well. Suzette enjoyed working with Greg even more, since they had talked. She had gained a greater sense of comeraderie.

Arriving home after the day's rehearsals, Suzette poured herself a tall glass of orange juice. She perched atop a barstool and kicked off her shoes. By her reckoning, it would take Fred another fifteen minutes to arrive at home. Her curiosity and concern had grown over the course of the afternoon. Fred seemed better in the afternoon, but he could have been faking it for the cast's sake.

The fifteen minutes crawled past. Finally Suzette picked up her lavender princess phone and dialed Fred's number.

The phone was ringing just as Fred walked up to the back porch. He fumbled with his keys, dropping them twice in his haste. Gaining the kitchen, he raced across the room and grabbed the wall phone receiver.

"Hello?" he gasped.

"Hello, Fred? Are you all right?"

"Oh, Suzette. . . yes, I'm. . . just out of breath." He recovered his composure. "I just got home."

Suzette laughed as he told her about the key dropping episode.

"So what did you need?" Fred tentatively queried. He had a sneaky suspicion what she wanted.

"I called to see how you're doing. You weren't quite yourself this morning, but it was pretty obvious that you didn't want to talk about it in public."

"No, I didn't, but what makes you think I'd like to talk about it now?"

"Nothing, just the concern of an old friend. And the fact that I know certain things about you that aren't common knowledge."

"Well, it's true that I have talked to you about it, sort of." Fred sighed. "I might as well tell you. But not on the phone. . ."

"I'll be there in twenty minutes."

"Thanks, Susie, I. . . well, even if it's difficult, I appreciate it. It's good to have you to confide in again."

After Suzette arrived, Fred still skirted the issue. Finally she confronted him.

"So tell me what's wrong."

Fred took a deep breath. "Do you remember the day we had lunch in my office?" Suzette nodded, so he went on. "I told you then that I only play the piano in private. Well, I did play for someone recently. Now he wants me to accompany him on his recital tour next fall."

Suzette waited quietly while Fred stared off into space, thinking. After he had gathered his thoughts, he continued, still looking into an abstract distance.

"I've heard of people falling in love with their accompanists, but to turn a lover *into* one. . . I've been seeing him off and on for two years, but this weekend was the first time I had ever played for him." Fred turned to face Suzette. "It's partly your fault, coming here and talking about old dreams, stirring up old fantasies. I never would have considered it a few weeks ago."

"I don't know whether to take that as a compliment or a derogatory remark." Suzette was disarmed when Fred began to chuckle.

"Here we are, a couple of old fools, wondering if our next step in life will shake the world."

They sat smiling ruefully at themselves, until Suzette brought them back to the topic at hand.

"Does your dilemma stem from the fact that this man is your lover? Or is it because opera directors aren't known for accompanying national recital tours?"

"Partly the first reason, I think, but mostly the second. It scares me that I want to do it so badly. I wouldn't have given the idea a second thought if you hadn't been talking about gaining our dreams. Dreams, plural. I'll never get my original dream. I'm not cut out to be a concert pianist. But to be a professional accompanist seems almost plausible."

"So where's the problem?"

"I haven't played in public for thirteen years. I don't know if I could do it. I'm not sure I'm up to it"

"If that day in your office was any indication, I'd say you've still got it. You played so much better than when I last heard you."

Fred nodded. "I have had a *few* lessons over the last thirteen years. . ."

"Let's assume that you are physically capable of doing it. Now what are your objections?"

"The time involved, for one thing. The tour would be during the time I usually spend planning the next season's productions. Then there is the fact that we've been lovers. I wouldn't mind continuing as lovers. But when you work too closely with someone, well, relationships tend to fall apart."

"And then it becomes difficult to continue the work," Suzette added. "I can see that becoming a problem. Maybe you should find someone else to accompany, someone who isn't too close to you."

"But then I would have to admit that the concert idea is a goal, and work at the arrangements. I'm not sure I'm willing to do that."

"So it really boils down to needing to make a commitment. That's something you'll have to decide for yourself, I'm afraid. Perhaps you should wait. Work hard on your playing for a few years, set up a tour farther in advance. . . what about this man's regular accompanist? Wouldn't his pianist be angry, to make a gross understatement?"

"Yes, there's that, too. She would not only be pissed as hell but she'd lose a lot of money as well. I'm well-off here. . .I have no reason to do that to anyone. I don't even want to. I guess I've just got itchy feet. First wanting to change the opera, and now wanting to run off and do a concert tour. . ."

"Sounds like a grown man's version of running off to join the circus."

"Running from one circus to another is more like it. Maybe I just need a vacation."

"Now there's an idea. Leave the opera in the hands of maestro Kleinemann for a few days. Or come down to my place for a weekend. Just a change of scenery helps sometimes. I'm not going down this weekend—Cass is coming up again—but I'll be going the next week. Think about it and let me know. Oh, and if you want to bring your friend, that's cool too."

"Thanks, Susie. . . I'll have to think about it." Fred sat quietly, until Susie broke into his thoughts again, changing the subject.

"Do you need any help with the party Wednesday? With the whole cast coming. . ."

"No, I hire caterers and maids for these things. I take them off my taxes as business expenses." Fred chuckled. "In a way it is a business expense. Having a pre-show party to keep my cast happy is an investment. It helps rehearsals to run more smoothly."

"I won't argue with that." Suzette thought about the day she had had to work so hard in rehearsal. She had been discontent, lonely for Cass. "Why didn't you tell me earlier that you have a lover? You only hinted about overnight guests—I didn't get the impression that one was a regular."

"I didn't tell you because we have a standing agreement. Neither of us will talk. . . at this point, our careers are more important. And like I said, it's been an off-again, on-again affair. We haven't been 'steady' these two years, just—kissing companions."

"May I assume also that this gentleman is a colleague of mine, since he has remained nameless?" Suzette had her suspicions. Greg's manner had seemed strange when he spoke of Fred.

"That's rather presumptuous of you, but yes, he is." Fred got up to refill their glasses. "And no, I will not now reveal his identity. By the way, how is Cass?"

"She's okay, last I heard."

"You don't sound convinced." Fred raised his voice as ice cubes crashed in the kitchen.

"It's just that we had a little tiff yesterday. We made up by the time she left, but these peevish little arguments leave a bad taste."

"I see. . . a little trouble in paradise." Fred returned humming.

"Why are you in such a good mood suddenly?"

He set the glasses brimming with Pepsi carefully on the coffee table before answering. "Because talking about my decision made me realize that there is no decision. I'm just fidgety. . . a concert tour is really out of the question. I'm not foot-loose and fancy-free, much as I like reminiscing about a time when we were. Talking to you tonight has helped me to realize a couple of things. First, that we aren't the same people that we were in college. And second, that as the person I am now, I have to live through my responsibilities. For now at least." He took a long draught of soda. "I'd love to join you for a weekend, though. If you don't think it would compound your marital problems."

"We'd be delighted to have you down." Suzette didn't add that his presence might prevent them from having another "tiff." "Fred, can I ask you another question?"

"Sure— shoot."

"How can you be so comfortable in the closet? Don't you hate lying to people?"

"Actually, I lie as little as possible. I simply refuse to discuss my private life with anyone. Except you, of course, but you're different. I knew you while I was coming out, when I was a young fool, not an old one. Later I knew I had to find a comfortable way of dealing with being gay in a straight world, without compromising my values. So I made a conscious decision. I've stood by it, too."

Suzette didn't say anything, but to her it still sounded like a lie. "I guess my values are a little different from yours." She could feel the years sitting on her shoulders, years of sinning by omission. "Suddenly I feel very old and tired. I think I'd better be going."

Driving home, Suzette pondered Fred's lifestyle. He had dealt with the world by not really dealing with the world at all. But he felt perfectly comfortable, knowing that he himself had made that decision. Perhaps making a specific decision, saying it aloud to herself, perhaps to Cass as well, would make her feel better. But in the back of her mind was a nagging, not words exactly, more a feeling. It felt unclean and made her thoughts itch.

When she arrived home, she put in a quick call to Cass. Suzette told her about the upcoming party on Wednesday, but said nothing about her discussion with Fred. It still needed to be sorted out. She wouldn't be comfortable until that nagging went away. At least she could forget about it while she was working. Actually she could keep it out of her mind most of the time, except when conversations or questions came up about her private life. For now her private life would have to remain private.

Tuesday's rehearsals went smoothly, all things considered. The talk of the day was Wednesday night's party. Gregory Loft and Margaret Byrd conspicuously discussed bringing their respective spouses. Greg seemed to have been reassured somehow about Fred, so Suzette didn't bring up the subject. Jennifer Doyle seemed more withdrawn than usual, which piqued Suzette's curiosity. The chorus buzzed with plans, forming carpools, talking about Fred's previous parties, etc. Even so, Act II got a good work-out. Maestro Kleinemann only called them down once. Fred also gave them one warning, but they could see his eyes smiling behind the stern mask. They respected him enough to keep it down until the breaks.

At lunch, Suzette cornered Jennifer. "Why are you so quiet today?"

"I'm just not sure I'm going to the party, that's all."

"Why ever not?"

"I don't have anyone to bring with me, and I don't want to be a wallflower. It's happened too often, and it's embarrassing." Suzette had become one of the few people Jennifer felt she could talk to. She had gotten over being in awe of her.

"Nonsense, you must come. It's opera protocol: singers must put in an appearance at all parties. Besides, I'm going alone, too. My other half can't come."

"Well, all right. Since you put it that way. We'd better go back—lunch is over." Jennifer dumped her trash in the nearest dome-topped receptacle and headed back to the stage area. She was interested in what Suzette had said about her "other half." Jennifer had had her suspicions about Suzette, and this was another definite indication. Married people don't usually refer to their spouses as their "other half." Maybe, just maybe. . . but no, she mustn't jump to any conclusions, much as she might enjoy doing so. She mustn't jeopardize herself.

The chorus had been dismissed before lunch. The afternoon rehearsal was dedicated to working out the delicate staging between Octavian and Sophie. Octavian enters and presents a silver rose to Sophie during an extended section of orchestral music. The length and grandeur of the music call for slow, graceful, courteous movements. Suzette had trained her body for years to acquire that grace. Without it, the scene would fall flat. It frequently did in other performances where the director left the responsibility of entertaining the audience up to the orchestra. The flow had to exist onstage as well.

Fred made Suzette go through the rose presentation again and again. Sometimes they would get to the actual singing before he stopped them. Finally they made it through the discussion of the perfume on the rose and the magical feeling of the moment.

"Good, good! You're both starting to get a real feeling for it! One more time, then we'll skip to the name section." Fred wanted to skip an interruption by the servants, since they were gone for the day.

Suzette went back upstage, past where there would eventually be doors. She took a few deep breaths to compose herself before the music began. She had found a long screwdriver backstage to use as the silver rose. Now she held it gently, letting it lay across her palms, her right hand slightly higher than the left. Stepping lightly on the balls of her feet, she moved slowly toward Sophie, seated in a chair. Sophie rose to meet Octavian as he flowed to her, each of them moving as though dancing a minuet. Their stylized movements lent a feeling of majesty to the scene. Octavian bowed deeply over the rose, his left foot sweeping slowly behind him in a circular movement. Sophie dropped a slow curtsey, then accepted the rose. They looked deep into each other's eyes. Suzette felt her heart pouring out to Sophie. Appropriate to the role, as they were supposed to fall in love, but unnerving to Suzette when she later realized what had happened. Jennifer, too, was caught in the thrill of the moment. It didn't matter that their silver rose was only an old screwdriver, nor that they were dressed in working clothes, not silver and white. The piano accompaniment sounded like the full orchestra to them, and their duet about the unforgettable wonder of that moment was sincere. Sincere, because at that moment it was real. At last they came to the place where Sophie's duenna takes the rose from her and places it in its case, so Fred reluctantly stopped them.

"That was magnificent! If you can do that every night, you'll bring down the house! Let's go on to the next bit."

Suzette knew that she could create a reasonable facsimile of that moment every night of the run, but it would never be quite the same. It would never again be real.

They went on to work out the next sequence involving only Sophie and Octavian. Sophie reveals her knowledge of Octavian's ridiculously long string of names. He laughingly remarks that she knows them better than he does himself! She also discusses her idealistic views on marriage, the man she is going to marry (whom she has never seen), and the entire Rofrano/Lerchenau clan. They marvel at each other for a while before the arrival of Baron Ochs and Sophie's father. There Fred stopped them again.

"It's getting late, and I've got to finish the party preparations. Let's go home! Good rehearsal, thanks." Fred dismissed them. "Please double check the call board before you leave," he shouted after them as they hurried down the hall, anxious to get home. Suzette and Jennifer obediently stopped to look at the next day's schedule, even though they already knew it by heart.

"Nope, no changes," Suzette said half to herself and half to Jennifer. "You sang well today."

"Thanks." Neither of them mentioned what had transpired on stage. Jennifer smiled inwardly. She was sure now. Suzette had to be a lesbian, too.

Chapter 7

Suzette rifled through the old wardrobe. She pushed aside another sequined gown with a sigh. Gertie jumped into the wardrobe, trying to be helpful.

"Come on, cat, get out of there. Maybe if we look later inspiration will strike."

She went down stairs, setting down her empty juice glass as she passed through the kitchen. The water in the bathtub gradually began to steam. Suzette eased herself into the bubbles with a sigh of pleasure. Parties were a lot of fun, but getting ready for them could be trying. She needed a few minutes to empty her mind. So many things had been going through her head lately— how to deal with Jennifer and Margaret, the small scene with Cass, Fred's problems— and the opera itself. The party should break up some of the tensions that had been building up in the last few weeks.

Finally Suzette drained the soothing water and rinsed the bubbles off her skin. She would have to hurry now. Being fashionably late is one thing, but missing half the party would be overdoing it.

Upstairs she selected a long gown, striking in its simplicity. The dress was of rough silk, the camel cloth covering her from neck to toes in the front. The silk draped lightly over her shoulders, forming a large V that dropped down in a breath-taking plunge to her waist. A sash of the same material circled her waist. Three loops of gold chain around her neck, designer shoes and a matching clutch completed the outfit.

"I guess I'm ready— if I've missed anything it's too bad," she thought to herself as she rushed out the door.

The party was in full swing when she arrived. The whole house was lit up like a Christmas tree. People seemed to be pouring out of every available door into the crisp night. The front porch and back patio were both crowded. Inside, a large group swarmed around the food and drink. Smaller amorphous groups shifted and changed throughout the long living room. Suzette moved through the group as though through parted waters, nodding and smiling to various chorus and crew members who gave way to her. Filling a plate at the loaded table, she looked around for Fred.

"Good evening."

"There you are, Suzette! I was afraid you weren't going to make it," Fred exclaimed, swimming over to her. "There are some people here that you *must* meet."

Suzette let herself be dragged across the room to meet a small clump of aging opera singers. They seemed only able to repeat the same stories of their past triumphs, without even the pleasant senile habit of elaborating each time. They had never been great, even in their prime. Mediocre artists only dull with age. Suzette said all the usual polite phrases and drifted away. Before she had a chance to reconnoiter, Margaret Byrd came swooping down upon her.

"Dah— ling, where have you been all evahning?"

Suzette eyed her warily, then smiled. Perhaps the party was a good time to get to know Margaret better. Rehearsals didn't give many opportunities for getting to know people. You only became acquainted with their acting, their singing, their rehearsal masks.

Suzette knew the Marschallin quite well already, but hardly knew Margaret at all.

Margaret looked stunning in her gown, tiny glass beads embroidered in large paisley patterns giving it a high sparkle. The flowing blues and greens set off her eyes. Suzette noted the daring scoop of the neckline, exposing the smooth inner curves of Margaret's breasts. Margaret Byrd was quite well preserved for her age.

Margaret placed her hand in the small of Suzette's back, guiding her to an empty corner. Her hand felt hot on Suzette's bare skin. "Dahling, we simply must talk."

They talked about rehearsals, singing, their respective careers—the usual small talk. Suzette couldn't get Fred's warning out of her head. He had told her to watch out for Margaret, and she had only half believed him. But after talking to her for a few minutes, Margaret did seem friendlier than when they had first met. Perhaps too friendly. *It must be my imagination. Fred's got me spooked, that's all.*

Finally Suzette caught a glimpse of Jennifer out of the corner of her eye. She managed to get away from Margaret slipping through the crowd to talk to Jennifer.

"Hello, Suzette. I didn't see you." Jennifer grabbed a canapé from a passing waiter.

"I've been trapped in boring conversations ever since I arrived," Suzette whispered conspiratorially. Aloud, she asked, "how are you this evening? We haven't had a chance to talk in a while."

"I'm fine. . . a little lonely, though. After all, my friends are still back in St. Louis."

"Surely you've made friends here by now," Suzette nudged gently.

"Only one or two, and I can't really talk to them about anything but singing."

"You mean there's more to life?"

Jennifer was taken aback until she noticed the twinkle in Suzette's eye. "Don't do that," she exclaimed, "you act too well. I'd never have kept a straight face," she murmured, half to herself.

"So tell me what else you like to talk about." Suzette was curious about this serious young woman.

"Oh, the usual things. Sex, mostly," Jennifer replied lightly.

"So now who's kidding?" Suzette laughed. "Although I suppose it's at least half true. Only most people won't admit it."

"Seriously, though, I noticed that Margaret had you cornered for a while over there. What did the old battle-axe want to talk about so badly?"

Suzette glanced over her shoulder at Margaret, partially concealed by the crowd. "She's hardly a battle-axe. But we really didn't talk about much." Suzette shivered as she remembered the lingering warmth of Margaret's hand on her body. *There goes my imagination again.*

"Well, I suppose I should circulate— I need to say hello to a few more people before I repeat the rounds to say good-bye!" Jennifer smiled warmly at Suzette and disappeared into the crowd.

The party thrived for several hours. Suzette found herself bouncing from one small group to another, meeting new people, greeting old. She knew that their chatter was as meaningless as hers. She stayed behind her mask of friendliness and watched the people as though they were animals in a zoo. She grew more and more detached, watching from the outside of the cage. She began to enjoy this peculiar form of voyeurism.

Her interest began to wane about the same time as the party. The crowd was slowly dissipating when Margaret found her again.

"Dahling, surely you're not leaving. . ."

"As a matter of fact, I am. I need my sleep if I'm going to be alert tomorrow. We do have rehearsal."

"Yes, I know," Margaret sighed. "And costume fittings as well."

"We have costume fittings tomorrow? I didn't know that."

"Oh, yes, it's posted on the call board. Didn't you check it today?"

"I confess I didn't— thanks for the warning. I really must be off now."

"Well, if you simply must. . . good night."

Suzette circled through the patio area saying her good-byes. Back inside, she found Fred.

"Good night, Fred. I've got to be going if I'm to be of use tomorrow."

"I think the party's winding down anyway. I noticed you talking to Margaret quite a bit. Have you survived the evening unscathed?"

"Yes, quite easily. No cutting remarks at all, really."

"That's not what I meant— you know that."

"I know, I was teasing you. But in fact, I did escape with my honor unharmed."

"Good, good. . . I'll see you tomorrow. Sleep well."

The next day Suzette stopped to look at the call board before going into the rehearsal. Jennifer was reading a note when Suzette walked up.

"Good morning. I see you survived the party."

Jennifer grinned. "That's only because I left early. You're looking pretty chipper yourself."

"I didn't know that 'chipper' was in the St. Louis vocabulary."

"It's not. At least, I'm the only one I know who says that."

"Ah, good, a non-conformist. My kind of person."

"You do seem rather non-conformist. . . maybe that's why you're such an interesting person."

"Thanks for the compliment. Actually I'm not a non-conformist by nature. I've been sort of forced into it."

"That's odd— I thought people would force you to conform, not the other way around."

Suzette chuckled. "That's usually the case, but I'm different. Paradoxical, isn't it?" She turned to look at the costume call notice. There— her time was at 2:00, during a chorus staging rehearsal. She'd be glad to miss that. Chorus staging rehearsals were characterized by general pandemonium.

Jennifer excused herself, hurrying to a coaching. *So she's "different." I wonder if she's as different as I think she is. If she is, I'd like to at least talk to her about it. But I suppose it really is to much to hope for. After all, how many opera stars can there be who are lesbians? Surely not that many. But then again, one in ten. . . or more, as near as I can tell.* She shook her head as if to clear her thoughts. She needed to concentrate on singing for a while.

Suzette arrived a few minutes early for her costume fitting. Gregory Loft was just handing his costume back to one of the designers.

"It's a good thing you're early," Greg told her. "They're running ahead of schedule. . . highly unusual, in this place." He smiled and went down the hallway towards the stage.

Suzette was wordlessly handed an assorted bundle of clothing. One of the costume people introduced herself and pointed out the dressing room.

"I'm Jill. If you need me, just yell."

Suzette was used to dressing in hoop skirts and petticoats, corsets and low-cut bodices. Now she found herself pulling on knickers and a ruffled shirt. She picked up an odd-looking piece of her costume and grimaced. Sticking her head out of the dressing room she called for Jill.

"Having trouble?"

"Don't tell me I have to wear one of these! That is, assuming it is what I think it is."

"I'm sure you've got it right. And yes, you have to wear it. It's period style." Jill was laughing as she went back to her sewing.

Suzette reluctantly closed the door and fastened on the cod-piece. She sighed. *First they give you a sword for the outside of the costume, and then they go and give you one for the inside! I guess that's the price you have to pay for playing a man.* Suzette finished dressing and stepped out into the costume shop.

Jill and one of the designers, Katie, began to pin and poke, pull and tuck. Suzette had plenty of time to look around the shop. Two rows of large sewing machines filled one end of the room. Bare mannequins stood in a far corner. The windows that ran the length of the room were hung with ferns and potted ivy. Long high tables were cluttered with costume pieces and various sewing notions, glue guns, fabric scraps, and cotton padding. Directly in front of Suzette were two mannequins dressed regally in Sophie and the Marschallin's finest attire. Around them were six wheeled hanging racks, heavy with costumes. The costumes were all in various states of completion, each hung neatly behind someone's name. The placard labeled "Etoile" had three different outfits below it—one for each act.

"Okay, now put on your boots. Here's a chair." Katie interrupted Suzette's inspection.

Suzette obediently pulled on the slick black boots as Jill pulled her hair back and tied it. "Your hair is a good length. We won't need to use a wig, except for Act II. We haven't made the wigs yet." Suzette stood up, trying out the new boots. "Now turn around."

Suzette obeyed again, then gasped. She was face-to-face with—Octavian. The big winged mirror af-

74

forded a view of each side as well as the front, and Suzette struck a cavalier pose, admiring her shapely legs in the knickers and knee-high boots.

"May I borrow the boots for rehearsal? And the sword," she added as they strapped the blade to her side.

"Of course—just bring them back every night."

Katie began marking hemlines and alterations with her pins and chalk. This gave Suzette the opportunity to scrutinize her costume. The heavy coat of deep blue velvet hung down to her knees, the square tails pulling away to expose her legs. The wide cuffs, richly decorated with gold embroidery, covered half of her forearm. A large ruffle flowed out of the top of her brocade waistcoat. Ice-blue satin knickers topping the sleek black boots completed the outfit.

When the alterations were marked, Jill helped Suzette out of her coat and sword. Suzette pulled the dress that would disguise her as a serving girl over her shirt and pants, and the chalk marking ritual was repeated. That done, her Act II costume was taken off the rack.

Pure white satin knickers replaced the ice-blue ones, and the black boots gave way to shiny white ones. The waistcoat was white on white, heavy embroidery giving it texture. Intricate silver designs covered her coat of snowy velvet.

The weight of each costume was considerable. Suzette was sweating by the time she got dressed in the white one. Fortunately it was the last costume she had to try on. She would wear the blue coat for both Act I and Act III.

Once again Katie began marking, first the coat, then the waistcoat. Having examined the room and its contents, Suzette found herself staring blankly into the mirror. She could see the racks of costumes and the half-open doors behind her. Suddenly movement in the mirror caught her eye. It was Margaret, coming in for her fitting.

I didn't realize she was after me. I was too busy talking to Jennifer to notice. I wonder what time it is now. . . I thought we were still running early. . .

Her reverie was interrupted when she felt Katie untying her shirt. "There are pins in your arm pits," she told Suzette matter-of-factly, "so we'll have to help you out of this. Careful!"

Almost before she knew what was happening, Suzette found herself standing bare-breasted in the middle of the costume shop. Glancing into the mirror, she saw Margaret standing with an armful of hoops and ruffles, staring openly at her. The tiniest of smiles played on her lips. Suzette looked away quickly, before Margaret saw her staring back. She turned and sat down to pull off her boots. *I'll give her something to look at!*

"Jill, could you help me with my boots? They're being stubborn."

Jill willingly went to her aid. Suzette placed her hands on the chair behind her hips to brace herself. She was careful not to let Jill get the boots off too quickly— she wanted Margaret to get a good look at her, if that was what she wanted. She tightened her pectoral muscles as she braced herself against Jill's tugging, purposefully showing off her breasts. Finally Jill got them off her feet. "Thanks Jill," was all she said before turning to go into the dressing room. She could feel Margaret's eyes on her back as she walked. One minute later Margaret joined her in the big dressing room. Much to Margaret's disappointment, however, Suzette had already slipped her blouse over her head. She finished fastening her slacks and was gone before Margaret had so much as undone a button.

Back out in the shop, Suzette relinquished her silver knickers. "You've done a lovely job with my costumes. I can't wait to see the rest of them. May I take the boots and sword now?"

"Certainly." Katie beamed at her. "Thanks for the compliment. I designed your costume myself." She busied herself with hanging up the satin pants. "You'll have one last fitting before dress parade. We may not have all the chorus costumes finished, but all the leads will have theirs. And don't forget to bring the boots back!" she called as Suzette headed out the door.

That night Cass called. "I tried to call last night but you weren't home."

"I was at the all-cast party. Out at Fred's."

"I didn't know there was a party last night. Why didn't you tell me?"

"I didn't think it mattered. It was in the middle of the week, so you couldn't have come up. Besides, you know we don't go to that kind of function together. Who knows what kinds of rumors would start flying?" Suzette was exasperated. They had been through this argument several times.

"That's beside the point. The point is that you haven't been letting me in on your life. You could have at least mentioned it!" Cass was feeling ignored. Susie always told her about her plans, her hard days, her hopes. It wasn't like her to act this way.

Suzette felt guilt twinging her stomach. *Now why should I feel this way? I haven't done anything wrong.* "Cass, I love you. It must have slipped my mind. I would have told you if I'd been thinking..."

"It slipped your mind? Since when has something as large as a party slipped your mind? You didn't forget to go, obviously! Sounds more like *I* slipped your mind." Cass was silent for a moment, stewing at the other end of the line. Suzette knew that no reply would be enough. Finally Cass spoke. "I guess there's nothing I can do about it now— or you, either. Nothing ever

77

gets solved on the phone. Just don't do it again!! Remember, you're attached to me, and it'll take an earthquake to change that. I love you, you know. I guess that's all I have to say tonight."

"I don't know what else I can say, either, except I'll try to do better. Are you still coming up here this weekend?. . . Great. I'll talk to you then. Goodnight, love." Suzette breathed a sigh of relief after replacing the receiver. There was no call to be so uptight. She hadn't done anything. Well, not really. The thought of Margaret in the costume shop that afternoon disturbed her. What did she want? Suzette had seen that expression before on women. She knew what it was like to be sought after by women and men alike. It was one of the advantages— and disadvantages— of her trade. And after Cass' tirade on the phone, it seemed blasphemous to even think about such things. Still, Suzette was intrigued. She had always wondered what it would be like, sleeping with a supposedly "straight" woman. Margaret was still a beautiful woman, despite her years. The dress she had worn to the party had been quite striking. Provocative, actually, would be a better description. But after all, it couldn't hurt to just look. Admiring other people is a very pleasant way to pass the time. Perhaps it was time to see another old Garbo flick. Suzette rummaged around in the pile of video cassettes under her TV. Not even the Crawford movies sounded appealing. Suzette sank down onto the couch, holding Gertie.

"Well Gertie, what do you suggest?"

The cat yawned and stretched in Susie's lap, settling in a comfortable curl.

"Thanks for the advice, cat. That's just what I need," Suzette told the sleepy cat as she carried her upstairs to bed.

Chapter 8

Friday evening came much too soon. Suzette was not looking forward to finishing their argument. Suzette had stopped for coffee with Fred after rehearsal, trying to delay the inevitable. She put off going home for as long as possible.

Driving up to the stately old house, Suzette saw Cass' small pickup in the side drive. As she unlocked the apartment door, she braced herself. Cass was probably lying in wait for her just inside the door.

To her surprise the living room was empty. Relief washed over her briefly, then her panicky anticipation returned. She was still tense, but she had made her entrance, played her part. Now it was Cass' turn. Suzette poured herself juice and sat down to wait.

After a few minutes she heard a rustle on the stairs behind her. Before she could turn, warm, bare arms wrapped around her neck. "It's about time you got home," Cass murmured into Susie's hair. The hands strayed down and began idly unbuttoning Susie's silk blouse. Suzette was startled. She had been expecting anything. . . except this. Susie barely managed to set her drink down on the glass coffee table before Cass had climbed over the back of the sofa.

"Cass, you're such a tease," Susie murmured as Cass' mouth avoided hers. Cass was a woman with a mission and she was not to be stopped. Her anger had slid under the surface of her skin, reappearing as tension. Cass meant to rid herself of that unwanted tension in the only way she knew. She intended to transfer it to its source— Suzette.

She slid the silk blouse ever-so-slowly off Susie's shoulders and down her slightly muscular arms. With one deft flick of her hand she unhooked Susie's bra, pushing it off with the lightest of fingertip touches. Susie's skin tingled. By now her nipples were awake, jumping to attention as Cass greeted each with a light flick of her tongue. But Cass moved on, slowly, deliberately. She unfastened the tiny gold buckle at Susie's waist and hooked her middle finger over the top of the zipper, teasing Susie's abdomen as she unzipped her slacks. Then Cass ran her hands down Susie's legs, gently slipping off her shoes, lingering just long enough to massage her toes for a moment. Then back up— Cass grabbed the top of her slacks and began insistently pulling them down. Susie lifted her buttocks from the sofa, almost thrusting them towards Cass, allowing the slacks to pass. Silent hands slid up the outside of her firm thighs and into the legs of her panties.

"I think the last piece can wait," Cass whispered. "No!" Susie's mind and body were screaming, but aloud she said nothing. Just a few minutes before, her body had been aching from a long day of rehearsals. Now it ached only for Cass.

Cass rose from her knees and bent over Susie, lips teasing lips. Then, at last, she kissed her full on the mouth, soft, moist, yielding. Her tongue teased, playing tag with Susie's. Suddenly the kiss became hard, insistent, surprising Susie with a rush of feeling. Cass ran her tongue quickly along the roof of Susie's mouth. Suzette tried to return the kiss, but Cass pushed her back. "Later," she whispered. Too weak to resist, Suzette gave in to her. Now Cass let her hot wet tongue leave a trail of dampness on Susie's body. Susie stifled a moan as Cass approached the hollow at the base of her neck. Cass worked her way back up to the flesh of her earlobe, pausing there to savor it a moment. Susie could barely control herself as the meandering tongue travelled down her body. When Cass reached her breasts, she began teasing again. She chewed lightly along the underside of the full roundness, causing Susie to arch her back. When her circular movements were getting close to the apex, Cass suddenly switched to the other breast.

"Ohhh!" Susie cried out at last, no longer able to contain herself. Satisfied, Cass let Susie have what she wanted: she took one nipple into her mouth and caressed it with her tongue. Susie cried out and gasped. Encouraged, Cass sucked harder, then grazed it with her teeth. Susie's body surged. "Now! Take me now," Susie begged, half screaming, half gasping. Cass teased her nipples a little more, enjoying a rush of power before obliging Susie. At last Cass gave in to Susie's desires, letting her new feeling of power transform into a desire to please, to satisfy Susie. Once she had begun the final move toward Susie's fulfillment, Cass began to succumb to an excitement of her own. Susie sensed Cass' excitement, realizing that the time to submit was over. They began to move together in a series of crescendos, finally reaching a huge sforzando. The last burst died down quickly and they both fell back exhausted.

"Mmm. . . that was wonderful, love. Thanks." Susie felt like purring, but decided she'd leave that to Gertie.

"Susie?" Cass sounded tentative.

"Mmm hmm?"

"I have a confession to make."

"Well, what is it?" Susie was becoming a little worried by the tone of Cass' voice.

"I. . . I'm afraid. . . I took advantage of you."

"What do you mean? I don't understand. . ."

"I was angry, and I wanted to take it out on you somehow. . ."

Susie remained silent, waiting for Cass to continue.

"So I made love to you like that. . . well, not at the end, but at first. . . I did that on purpose."

Suzette was beginning to understand. They had never made love in quite the same way before. In general their lovemaking was mutual. They had had few one-sided love sessions previously. They had stemmed from tiredness or occasionally the desire of one woman not to be touched for some reason. But today there had been a different feeling. Now that Suzette looked back on it, she could see it.

"Do you mean you used sex against me instead of facing our problems? That's awfully low."

Cass nodded silently, obviously unhappy with the whole situation.

"Well, I hope you're satisfied."

"Actually, I'm not. I. . ."

"Yes? Go on," Suzette prodded.

"I'm sorry. There, I said it." Cass turned away.

"We still haven't dealt with Thursday's argument."

"I know, but I'm not angry any more. At least part of my plan worked— I got rid of a lot of anger. Now I'm just sorry I did it the way I did. Can't we just forget about the whole thing?" She smiled ruefully at Susie.

"Easier said than done. I'm feeling a little bruised." Suzette smiled. "I'll try not to think about it for a while, if that's what you want."

Cass sighed. "I know I handled things badly, but I'm through being angry over last week. I'd rather call the whole thing off— shake hands and start over."

"How about kiss and make up? That sounds like more fun to me."

Cass laughed. It seemed to her that Susie was willing to forgive and forget. Susie did forgive Cass, but she wasn't so sure that the original argument should be forgotten. The argument had passed for the night, at least, but she knew it would keep cropping up until it was finally resolved. She turned away from these unwelcome thoughts and back to her lover.

After a light dinner they climbed the stairs to bed. They settled into each other's naked arms again with a sigh of relief, the sigh of their skin's thirst being quenched. They held each other for a long time, stroking sensuously but without sexual intent. They simply wanted the warmth and comfort of human contact. This was a subtler need, a calmer though perhaps more urgent physical necessity than the quick release of sexual desire in orgasm.

Sunlight streaming warm across their naked bodies woke them the next morning. Susie was the first to awaken, her body being on an early morning schedule for the opera. She bent and kissed Cass lightly on the shoulder, making her stir.

Cass smiled up at Susie. "Morning."

"Good morning, love. What would you like to do today? Stay home with me?"

"Actually, if you wouldn't mind, I'd like to do a little sight-seeing. Or maybe shopping. . . something outside, at any rate. I haven't really had a chance to look the place over."

"I know just where to go. We'll do the town!"

Susie had a great time leading Cass all over town. They browsed through the antique stores where Suzette had bought her bedroom furniture. When they arrived in the shop that had sold Suzette the gold pocketwatch, Cass proudly displayed the now-ticking watch to the shop owner.

"Looks good— must have cost a pretty penny to fix it."

"It was worth it. Do you have a fob that would go well with it?"

Suzette had to settle for a battered old fob, but Cass seemed pleased. When they got back out on the street, Cass gave her a quick peck on the cheek. Her shining eyes showed how much the gift was appreciated.

"It's a little worn, but I don't mind. You know watch fobs are hard to find these days, especially antiques. I've always wanted one of these," she exclaimed, weighing the metal in her hand before hooking it onto the watch. "Now I'll have to get a proper waistcoat to wear it on!"

Suzette laughed. "You could borrow one of mine, but I think the costume people would object." Over hot dogs in the park, Suzette told Cass all about her costume fitting. All, that is, except the incident with Margaret. No need to spoil a beautiful day, Suzette reasoned.

They spent the afternoon playing like little kids in the park. Susie loved to swing. She found the motion very soothing, not unlike the comfort of a rocking chair. Gradually she relaxed, until Cass was able to coax her into a little competition. They tied in their effort to see who could swing highest.

Finally Cass got bored and jumped out of her swing, running to the little merry-go-round. Susie sighed and followed at a more sedate pace. Cass was in a silly mood again, so she might as well go along.

Cass ran with the merry-go-round and jumped on it, leaving Susie laughing and making faces still on solid ground. Cass got tired of teasing her, so she slowed down for Susie to join her. Susie hopped on, glad to rejoin Cass. Cass decided to make the merry-go-round spin as fast as she was able, so she ran with it until Susie cried for mercy.

"Let me off this thing!" Suzette sat down on the ground, hard. "I'm so dizzy I can't stand," she told

Cass, laughing. She was beginning to get into the spirit of the day.

"I always knew you were just another dizzy soprano," Cass teased.

"We'll see about that— race you to the see-saw!" she called, deciding to give Cass a taste of her own medicine. She took off running before Cass had a chance to jump to her feet. Cass tore off after her, catching her around the waist just after she tagged the see-saw. "I beat," Susie whooped.

Susie climbed on the teeter-totter first, holding it level for Cass. Just as Cass straddled the board, Susie pushed her end down quickly. The other end whacked Cass in the butt.

"I'll get you for that, Eaton!" Cass howled. Then Cass sat down quickly, keeping Susie suspended in mid-air. The two women were near equals in weight, but Cass did have a slight advantage.

"Hey, let me down!" Susie kicked her feet forcefully, but to no avail.

"That's just like you, Miss Eaton. Always wanting something." Cass laughed, then pushed up from the ground with her feet. They teeter-tottered peacefully for a while, then suddenly Susie stopped at ground level. She had had an urge to beat Cass at her own game. If Cass could be a child for the day, so could she.

"I don't want to play this game anymore," she said petulantly, imitating a small child's voice. Very carefully she got off her end, holding it down with her hands. Then without notice she let go. Cass hit the ground with a bang.

"Ow! That's not fair!"

"All's fair in love and teeter-totters," Susie flung over her shoulder as she ran back to the swings.

When Cass reached the swings, she found a more serious Susie.

"What's wrong?"

"Nothing, I'm just tired. I think I'm ready to go home. . . I've played out at least a month's worth of wild abandon."

Cass sat heavily in the next swing. "Me too. . . but I've had a fun day. I sure like playing with you. It seems to be kind of rare these days. It's enough to make me want to preserve today under glass."

"Like a pheasant?" Suzette laughed at herself. "I must be getting hungry, to be making bad food puns."

"Let's go home and change. I want to go someplace nice for dinner."

"Okay— I know just the place. Are you ready to be served in style?"

"Dahling, I'm *always* ready to be served. Period."

Suzette laughed uneasily. Cass in her playfulness had sounded disturbingly like Margaret Byrd.

Getting back to the apartment, they went upstairs to change. Undressing came perilously close to being their downfall. They clowned around, still as playful as kids, taking off pieces of each other's clothing. Suddenly Cass got behind Susie and grabbed her with one arm, slowly unfastening her jeans with one hand. Suzette squirmed out of her arms, whirling to grab the tail of Cass' shirt. Before Cass could blink twice, Susie had pulled her shirt off over head.

"So that's the way you want to play, eh?" Cass inquired rhetorically, diving for Susie. She caught her full around the waist and threw her on the bed.

"Hey, watch it! What are you trying to do to me?" Suzette protested as Cass ripped the bluejeans off her body.

"I'm getting tit for tat," Cass replied as she deftly unhooked Suzette's bra and took her breasts into her hands. Susie moaned at the bad pun. Then her moan sharpened as Cass took her nipple into her teeth.

When Cass took her mouth away to inquire, "Like it?" Susie wrenched away.

"You know I do, but I'm too hungry to play like that now! Come on, let's get dressed."

Reluctantly Cass agreed. As she began to pull on a pair of sheer pantyhose, she thought back on the silliness of the day. *It's been a long time since we've played together like that. I think the day in the park did me more good than last night. . .*

"Hey, whatcha thinking about so serious?" Suzette was struck by Cass' sudden silence and somber expression.

"Oh, nothing. Just thinking that I like playing with you, that's all. So where are we going for dinner?"

"I can't tell you that. It's a surprise!" Suzette grinned to herself. She knew Cass would love The Olive Tree.

"Great! I love surprises," Cass said, pleased that Susie wanted to continue the games. "Is it romantic? Can I gaze into your eyes across the table?"

"Of course. That is, as long as I can gaze back. Hurry up! I'm practically starved." Suzette finished throwing odds and ends into a purse and stood waiting for Cass to put on her shoes.

"When was the last time we did this?" Cass asked, trying to distract her attention and keep her from growing impatient.

"You mean, gaze into one another's eyes? Far too long."

"No, silly thing, I meant going out to dinner in a fancy restaurant— on a date, that is— just you and me?"

"Wasn't it a couple of weeks ago, just before I came up here?"

"No, that was with Sally and Julia. Remember?"

"Wait— it's all coming back to me now," Susie said, her eyes closed and the fingers of one hand pressed to her forehead. "I was so absorbed in your great beauty that I was oblivious to any other presence. But no, I feel shadows nearby, very dim. . . growing stronger, brighter. . . one is. . . one is. . . yes, one is Sally. And with her. . . Julia!" Suzette finished triumphantly just before Cass tackled her, laughing.

"Oh, woman!"

"Careful! You'll wrinkle us!" Suzette cried. Righting themselves, they finally made it out the door, still laughing.

Suzette managed to park around the corner from the restaurant. Even though it was still early, the small parking lot was packed with cars. The two women exchanged a quick kiss in the murky dusk before going up to the front door.

The Olive Tree was a quaint old house that the owners had renovated, rather than destroying it and starting fresh. The front door, a dark affair with a large oval of etched glass in the center, swung open to reveal a small entryway, complete with an elaborate umbrella stand. A "Please Wait to Be Seated" sign pointed the way into a tiny parlor filled with sofas and overstuffed chairs.

"So far so good. . . I like it. How did you find this place?" asked Cass, flopping down on a ball-and-claw legged sofa.

Suzette sat primly in a big wing chair. "Fred told me about it. I've only eaten here once, but it was wonderful. Fred knew I would like it. After all, it's owned and operated by a couple of lesbians. I'm not sure, but I think most of the waitpeople and kitchen staff are lesbians, too."

"All lesbians! Wow, gourmet lesbians. Now I really like this place. I can hardly wait to taste the food!" Cass laughed, her pleasure sparkling off the crystal.

"I knew you would." Suzette beamed, quite pleased with herself.

After a short time the hostess came in to seat them. "Non-smoking, please," Suzette replied to her inquiry.

They were led to a small room where several other couples were at various stages of their dinner. Each table had a fine white vase of bone china that held a single flower. Suzette and Cass were seated at a table by the window.

Cass took one look out the window and grinned. "What a lovely view!"

"Of course. Nothing but the best for you, love. That's the garden where they grow their own vegetables. They have a hot house, too, out back." Suzette snapped the folds out of her napkin before spreading it on her lap.

"That explains the baby asparagus on the menu." Cass had turned her attention to the list of culinary delights.

The waitress returned three times before they were both ready to order. Suzette teased Cass a little— "It's a menu, not a hot sex mag." Finally Cass reached a decision.

"I'll have the boeuf moutard and the artichoke fritters, please."

"What, no appetizer?" Suzette asked in mock horror.

"Of course not." Cass leaned conspiratorially over the table and whispered, "I'll just eat some of yours."

The waitress cleared her throat as though impatient, but Cass noticed a knowing gleam in her eye. Suzette ignored Cass' remark and turned to the waitress.

"I'll have the cashew mushroom stroganoff." She ordered a bottle of wine, and the waitress hurried away. "Nice legs," she whispered to Cass, still teasing.

Cass sighed. "It's hopeless. You'll just never be politically correct. Maybe I should give up trying." She took a sip of ice water to cover her smile. "Besides, she does have nice legs. It's been a long time since I've seen a waitress in sensible flat shoes, that's why I noticed," she added quickly to block the retort forming in Suzette's mind.

Before Susie could reply the woman reappeared with the wine. Without hesitation she extended the bottle to Cass.

After they had been served and the waitress retired to the kitchen again, Cass whispered fiercely to Susie, "Why did she do that? *You* ordered the wine. . ."

"Yes, dear, but you look butcher than I do, in spite of your dress." She couldn't resist a little dig. "Perhaps it seemed to her to be more politically correct to let you taste the wine."

Cass just stewed for a moment, then decided to dismiss it. "Let's have a toast. To Octavian!"

"And to the *Magic Flute* set!" Suzette raised her glass to Cass' current project. "And to us," she whispered with a meaningful look at Cass. Cass smiled, and crystal clinked crystal.

The food took all their concentration during dinner. But finally they each finished their last morsel, laying down their forks.

Cass sighed happily. "I'm awfully full, but I sure would like to try that mocha hazelnut souffle."

"Then do it. If you can't finish it, we'll take it home." Suzette hailed the waitress, ordering two servings and coffee.

"Mmm. . . the perfect topping for a wonderful day," Cass said blissfully after her first bite.

"I'd better get you home while you've still got that look on your face," Susie told her half-jokingly. "I'd like to take advantage of it."

"Oh, woman," Cass replied, "you can find it again. And you know it," she added, smiling slyly.

When they got back to Susie's apartment, she did find it again. Long slow caresses brought blissful smiles to both their faces. Fully relaxed, they slipped easily into a dreamless sleep.

They awoke late the next morning, and regretfully got out of bed. Cass had to leave early because she was behind schedule at work. They dawdled over brunch, trying to prolong the weekend. Finally Susie gave Cass a tender farewell kiss, and they went their separate ways. Cass headed out of town, while Suzette drove to MacAlister Community College. Suzette was running away temporarily from her conspicuously empty apartment, the opera house, and the opera. She wanted to practice some art songs that she hadn't worked on in weeks instead of going over her role "just one more time." At the Community College she would be an anonymous singer in a small room for several hours. The thought of getting away from herself for a while was suddenly appealing.

Chapter 9

Monday, Suzette hummed as she went through her morning routine. She felt refreshed from her weekend with Cass, even though it had ended early. The time to herself, singing for her own pleasure, made her feel good, too. It was a rare treat when she was in the middle of an opera. Singing just for fun had a freeing effect on Suzette. It made her opera singing, the singing she had to do, much more relaxed. It also set her mind free. She was able to transcend her daily problems or augment her pleasures. Sunday it had been the latter.

Pulling open the heavy stage door, Suzette walked proudly onto the stage. She joined Fred, who had been the first to arrive.

"You're in high form this morning. Do I detect an extra lilt in your step?" Fred smiled.

"Perhaps." Suzette smiled back, rather coyly.

"Come now. You know I won't be satisfied until I get details!"

"I guess you'll never find satisfaction, then. There really are no details—I just had a particularly good weekend, that's all." Suzette's smile was no longer coy—only kind.

Fred quickly double-checked to be sure they were alone. "With Cass?"

"Of course." Suzette had noticed Fred's sharp glance around the stage area. It was one more tiny reminder of her closet. Suzette decided not to let it bother her. She didn't want to lose her weekend high, not yet.

A few minutes later Margaret and the pianist arrived and the rehearsal began. They were working to polish the opening scene of Act I, between Octavian and the Marschallin. Suzette and Margaret took their places on the big four-post bed that the stage crew had set the night before. The scene shop had just finished it. Every day a few rehearsal props and temporary stage pieces were being replaced by the real props and furniture. This gave the stage a strange look, as though it were a caterpillar in a transparent cocoon, seen in the midst of its metamorphosis. The full butterfly would be finished late the next week, just in time for dress rehearsals.

Margaret and Suzette took a few moments to familiarize themselves with the bed and the other new set pieces, walking quickly through their staging once, without music. Then Suzette returned her sword to the chair and they settled themselves to begin in earnest.

Margaret, the Marschallin, was lying in the big bed. A gauzy curtain, though tied back, partially concealed her. Octavian knelt on a footstool beside her, proclaiming his love.

The rehearsal proceeded fitfully. Fred made them work small sections at a time, smoothing out the details. At last they had worked their way up to the entrance of Baron Ochs.

"Okay, now I want you to take it from the top. I won't stop you this time," Fred instructed, "so I want you to play it as though it were real. *Feel* it. You are no longer opera singers. You are lovers, having a lovely morning together, and whatever happens during the course of the morning just happens. Experiment, have fun with it." He added: "Obviously you have to keep your wits about you for performances. But for now I want you to abandon yourselves. . . I want you to get a real feeling for the scene, so you can reproduce it later." He nodded to the pianist, and they began again.

Suzette found it easy to let herself go this morning. Her fine mood had stayed with her through the more tedious portion of the rehearsal, so it seemed natural to enjoy playing the full scene.

Octavian held the Marschallin in their opening embrace, waiting for the music to reach the curtain cue. Suzette felt herself sinking simultaneously into the music and Margaret's soft body, immobile on the bed. Then the music became part of her being, part of Octavian. It was no longer flowing into her body, but out of it.

"Wie Du warst! Wie Du bist! Das weiss niemand, das ahnt Keiner!" she sang to the Marschallin, pouring out the words effusively. These were the words of a young boy after a night of love. Suzette was years past youth, years past first love, but she knew the joys of her lover's arms.

The Marschallin balanced Octavian's bubbling outbursts with quiet simplicity. Her soft exclamations shimmered with tenderness. "Du bist mein Bub, Du bist mein Schatz!" she sang, her eyes shining playfully, then adding softly: "Ich hab' Dich lieb!" Margaret's "I love you" was quite ardent.

Suzette felt Margaret leaning into their embrace with an unaccustomed fervor. Octavian, anxious to keep the Marschallin to himself, pulled away to protest the coming day. Daylight meant that Octavian must leave; the Marschallin's boudoir was not really his domain. Margaret seemed genuinely amused at Suzette's discomfort when a small bell rang. She knew it was her servant with breakfast, but Octavian thought it might be a messenger bringing letters from other suitors. Octavian was loathe to admit any intruder, yet powerless to prevent them. At last a small boy came in with breakfast, and Octavian slipped quickly out of sight behind the screen.

The Marschallin chided Octavian for leaving his sword lying around in a lady's bedroom, but over breakfast they became very tender once more. Suzette and Margaret's exchange of pet names was much more gentle than it had been, each name said almost as though with real love:

Sincerely: "Marie Theres'!"

"Octavian!"

Then tenderly: "Bichette!"

"Quinquin!"

And playfully: "Mein Schatz!"

"Mein Bub!"

Suzette felt a lovely warmth sitting at the little table with Margaret. Today it was very easy to play off of her. When they had first begun rehearsals, Suzette had found Margaret as cold and hard as stone. Margaret would go through the motions she had been instructed to use, very graceful but unyielding. She had been gradually softening, but today for the first time she seemed actually pliable. Every nuance in Suzette's voice or body movements was received and answered by Margaret. Thus encouraged, Suzette became bolder in her performance.

Suzette was enjoying herself immensely until the Marschallin sang that she had dreamt of her husband, the Feldmarschall, in the night. Octavian became distressed at the thought of the Marschallin dreaming of anyone else, especially the very night they had been together. Worse still, it wasn't just anyone, but the Marschallin's husband, the last person Octavian wanted to remember. Then their attention was drawn to noises in the courtyard, sounds of horses. With thoughts of the Feldmarschall still fresh, they believed he had returned. Octavian tried to convince the Marschallin that it couldn't be him, he was far away on a hunting trip. But no, he travels like the wind. . . Suzette felt real jealousy welling up inside her when the Marschallin began to say something about "einmal. . .," when the Feldmarschall had come home unexpectedly. With true urgency Octavian tried to discover what had happened, but the Marschallin wisely would not say. Finally the Marschallin was convinced that it was her husband, but all avenues of escape had been cut off for Octavian. After much delay and indecision, after expressing concern for the Marschallin if she were caught with Octavian in her room, Octavian hid behind the screen. The Marschallin, with a surprising display of spunk, prepared to make a stand against her husband. But as she listened, she realized that the voice outside her private entrance didn't belong to her husband, but rather to her cousin, Baron Ochs. Relief and gaiety flooded through her and she laughed about it to Octavian, still hidden.

Fred sang the lines of the Major-Domo and Baron Ochs, unseen outside the Marschallin's boudoir. The Baron was trying to burst into the room and the Major-Domo was trying valiantly to keep him out. Fred didn't want to stop Suzette and Margaret until the last possible moment. He was amazed at their transformation on the stage. It was obvious to him that they had taken his instructions to heart. They seemed to have entirely forgotten that they were really Suzette Etoile and Margaret Byrd.

After hearing the Baron trying to enter, Margaret called out for "Quinquin." Octavian reappeared from behind the screen, dressed in a skirt with a kerchief around his head. He sang to her in the idiomatic

German of a servant girl, his voice high and light. Amused, the Marschallin gave Octavian a kiss for his wages. It was just a small peck, but Suzette felt a thrill run through her body at the touch. Then Octavian went to try to escape through the small door.

"That's enough!" Fred called out to stop them just when the Baron should have burst through the small door, bumping into Octavian. Suzette and Margaret both jumped slightly. They hadn't been prepared for the abrupt jolt back to reality. Suzette shook her head to clear it. It took both women a minute to recover themselves.

"That was excellent," Fred told them. "I wish we had done this a week ago! Now I think you have a real feel for what's going on here. Any questions or comments? No? Okay, break time."

Suzette hurried off the stage. She didn't want to talk to Fred. She wanted to be alone to sort out her thoughts.

Grabbing a cup of stale coffee, Suzette went outside. She pulled her jacket close around her shoulders. Fall weather had come late, but when it arrived it did so with a vengeance. Even the cup of coffee failed to keep Suzette's hands warm, but she didn't notice. Her mind was whirling with thoughts of Margaret. She had to admit that she had enjoyed showing off her body in the costume shop that day. And today. . . she wasn't sure *what* had happened, she was only sure that *something* had happened. That intangible something had happened to Margaret, too. Suzette was sure of it. Never before had Margaret yielded so willingly to her embraces. And throughout the breakfast scene Suzette had felt a tangible warmth coming from Margaret's eyes. Suzette might have been convinced that her performance earlier had been just that, a performance, if Margaret's acting skills were more than just average. *No, her "performance" had to* *have been real. I guess the only thing to do now is wait and see if anything comes of all this. It's hard to admit, but... well... she **is** an attractive woman. I'm not sure I could block any advances... I'm not sure I'd want to. I don't want to just cop out and ignore the situation, but how can I make a rational decision on an irrational subject? Besides, what if nothing happens? Then I'll have made a big fuss over nothing. That's probably all that **will** happen—exactly nothing.*

Having dismissed the subject, Suzette went back inside the theater. The rest of the day was spent working through Act II, in which the Marschallin does not appear. Suzette thought at first that it was best not to see Margaret for the rest of the day. She discovered, however, that in her lovely intimate scene with Sophie she was not thinking of Jennifer, but of Margaret. *Why, when I have this beautiful young woman in front of me, when I am singing of love to Jennifer, why am I seeing Margaret? Why doesn't out of sight mean out of mind?*

Later, when Suzette was safe at home, she was still plagued by thoughts of Margaret. How could she face her the next day? But she had had a tender moment on stage with Jennifer, too, last week. Nothing had happened after that. The best thing was to pretend that it had never happened.

Unfortunately Suzette overlooked some basic differences between Jennifer and Margaret. Jennifer was young. She was just getting started on her career. Margaret on the other hand was older, more jaded. Her career, though she would never admit it, was drawing to a close.

By Tuesday morning Suzette had put the incident out of her mind, but a queasy feeling in her stomach remained. She stopped to initial the sign-in sheet just as the door leading to the house swung shut. *Great. I'm in no mood for an audience today.*

Jennifer settled into one of the plush auditorium seats, letting it rock backwards. It would have been nice to sleep late, but she was curious to see the first act. She knew that Act III would make more sense after she had developed a sense of continuity. She knew the plot of the whole opera, but knowing it and seeing it were quite different. For one thing, the interpretations of the characters by Margaret, Suzette, and Gregory would be unique. Besides, it was a treat to see Suzette in action. Jennifer would never admit it to her face, but she found Suzette intriguing. Plus it warmed her heart to see respected lesbians. After all, wasn't she herself striving to be a successful opera singer?

Jennifer's thoughts were interrupted by the opening strains of Act I. Even without the orchestra, the rich harmonies of Richard Strauss began to seep into her bones. She sighed with pleasure, closing her eyes and letting the music ripple through her body. *I'll never tire of this opera.*

The curtain rose to reveal the giant bed, draped in heavy multi-colored tapestry and hung with huge gold tassels. Sort of half in and half behind the bed Jennifer could see Suzette, bending over someone. The person hidden by the drapes was, Jennifer knew, Margaret Byrd. Jennifer smiled to herself. *I'm going to enjoy this. Watching love scenes between two women has always been one of my favorite pastimes.* She looked Suzette up and down appreciatively. *Especially when one of the women is so attractive!*

As the scene progressed, Jennifer began to sink back into the music momentarily. Suzette was singing beautifully, and Margaret was rising to match her. But after Margaret rose from the bed, Jennifer's attention was drawn to tiny details. The brushing of a hand, a surreptitious glance, the peculiar twist in a smile— these things would have seemed a part of the acting to a casual observer. But Jennifer was, as an observer, seldom casual. She was usually analyzing, hoping to learn. What she saw in those gestures was the impression of reality.

Surely I'm making this up. No one in their right mind would fall for Margaret. But then again. . . she **is** *a beautiful woman.* Jennifer smiled appreciatively at Margaret's wispy garb. *I suppose it is possible. And those gestures. . . but the way they're touching each other. . . I can't be mistaken!*

Jennifer sat on the edge of her seat for the rest of the act, scrutinizing every move Suzette and Margaret made. There was no doubt about it. Their interaction with Baron Ochs, the servants, the crowd of people who rush in to petition the Marschallin for money—none of it had the same eerie sense of reality. On the other hand, Suzette and Margaret seemed to become more enamored of each other, and more furtive in their expression of it. All perfectly legitimate in the plot, but still it made Jennifer uncomfortable somehow. She leaned forward to watch the last scene, after the hairdresser, orphans, Baron Ochs, et al have exited. Somehow Margaret was less convincing when the Marschallin sings of her melancholia, her fear of aging. She knows that Octavian will not always be hers. Margaret, on the other hand, could not quite conceal her obvious triumph. She looked like she was about to get just what she wanted— and it didn't seem to be eternal love. Margaret's face wore a sad mask, but behind it her eyes sparkled. Jennifer detected a slight flush in her cheeks beneath the heavy make-up. Jennifer frowned at Margaret's unrestrained infatuation, partly because it was, at least momentarily, out of character. Suzette remained in character, but it was easier for her. Octavian was doing his best to convince the Marschallin that he would never leave her. Appropriately enough, Suzette's advances were as ardent as ever.

Jennifer felt slightly nauseous by the time the curtain dropped. The sick feeling hadn't gone away by the time she reached the room where she was to have a coaching. *There's definitely trouble brewing... I wish there were some way to caution Suzette. Margaret's sure to be bad news.*

As she began to sing, Jennifer's mind gradually settled on her work. By the time she had sung her third phrase, she had forgotten the alarms in her stomach. Suzette would just have to watch out for herself.

Chapter 10

Margaret knew that Suzette would be waiting in the wings when the curtain went down. After that run of Act I, Suzette was right where she wanted her. Smiling at Suzette, Margaret brushed past her, counting on Suzette to follow. She led her into the nearest dressing room. They both knew that Fred would have notes for them, but Margaret hoped to have a few minutes before they were missed. Right now she had to seal her hold on Suzette. The time was right.

When they reached the dressing room, Margaret closed the door quietly behind them. Without a word, she pulled Suzette to her. Their kiss was long and passionate.

"Lunch. My place. After notes." With that, Margaret was gone.

Suzette dropped onto a chair to catch her breath. Things had definitely gone too far for her to turn back. The most frightening aspect was the fact that the seduction had taken place, almost literally, in the spotlight. Her only consolation was that no one would have noticed. Except Fred. She would need someone to talk to about all this. Perhaps it was just as well that he probably already knew. He just wouldn't know how far things had gone— at least, not until she had told him.

The drive to Margaret's apartment was short. Suzette distracted herself with thoughts of the light drizzle dampening the road, the ease with which they would get back in time for their afternoon rehearsal—thoughts of anything but where she was going, and why.

Suzette arrived at Margaret's too quickly for her common sense to regain control. She saw Margaret's silver Volvo in the parking lot, and sighed with relief. If Margaret hadn't arrived first, she might have turned and fled. Suzette was drawn by Margaret's charms, and she knew that she would not rest easy, not be satisfied, until something tangible happened. Now something was going to happen, and Suzette's rational side seemed powerless to prevent it.

Margaret waited a few seconds before opening the door. She didn't want to seem overeager. She had to maintain her image of collectedness even in the midst of passion.

"Do come in." Margaret smiled a rare smile at Suzette. "Make yourself comfortable." Her words were significantly weighted in what Margaret considered a suggestive manner. She headed for the kitchen to fix herself a martini. "Care for a drink?"

"No thanks. More singing this afternoon."

"Don't remind me." Margaret returned, her glass half empty by the time she reached the sofa. She sat gracefully down next to Suzette. Martini in one hand, she cupped Suzette's chin with the other. "I'm so glad you've come. I do hope you will come again, soon."

Suzette's mind groaned at the bad pun, but her body tingled. Every moment that Margaret delayed increased both Suzette's dread and her excitement. But Margaret was through delaying. Tugging gently on Suzette's chin, she guided their lips together in a kiss. Suzette yielded, letting herself sink into Margaret's arms.

"Let's go somewhere more comfortable, dahling," Margaret purred. Victory was so near she could taste it. It was all she could do to keep from trembling with nervous excitement. She had seduced many men in her time, but no women. Well, not since college, but that didn't really count. She hadn't had much experience then. Besides, everyone was a little wild in college, away from home for the first time. One could overlook such trifles. Now, however, was a different matter. She wanted to know if women were as hot in bed as her male lovers always claimed. Besides, men were becoming boring, predictable. Margaret let her hand stray to Suzette's blouse.

Suzette almost moaned as Margaret undid the top button of her blouse. She was willing to let Margaret call the shots, but it took great control. Suzette held her breath. With every button that gave way, her body gained more control over her mind. Finally her last remnants of resistance gave way as Margaret's hand slipped inside to caress her skin. Suzette collapsed into Margaret's arms, kissing her neck.

"Careful, dahling, no marks!" Margaret laughed as she set her empty glass down. "Come with me."

Slipping one arm around Suzette, Margaret led her to the master bedroom. Sitting on the edge of the king-sized bed, Margaret pulled Suzette down to her. "Now we'll really know what that first scene feels like, you and I."

There was no more time for talking, no more need for it. Margaret skilfully removed Suzette's clothes, but slipped out of her own before Suzette had a chance to lift a finger. Not bothering to pull down the bedclothes, the two women sank down onto the satin coverlet. Another kiss insured their passion. Margaret, however, relinquished her command. She obviously expected Suzette to take the lead now. Willing to please, Suzette cupped Margaret's breast in her hand, rolling it between her hand and her cheek. She drank in Margaret's scent, her perfume of musty dried flowers. When Suzette turned to drink of the breast itself, Margaret moaned and twisted under her. Smiling to herself, Suzette continued stroking Margaret's body until Margaret screamed for mercy.

"Please. . ." Margaret could not utter another word. Suzette knew what she wanted though, or thought she did. Sliding her body down between Margaret's knees, Suzette let her fingers play briefly in the tightly curled hair that surrounded her goal. Then swiftly she brought her tongue into play. Margaret squirmed, then pushed Suzette's head away from that sensitive area.

"No—your hands."

Undaunted, Suzette obliged. Sliding her hand through Margaret's furry wetness, she pulled herself up onto her knees. Margaret flung one arm over her eyes, as though to keep Suzette from reading her emotions. As Suzette slid first one finger, then several, into Margaret's cavernous womb, Margaret grunted in pleasure. Glad to have found the key to Margaret's desire, Suzette slipped in the last of her fingers. She was amazed at Margaret's depth. Using her thumb, Suzette began playing with Margaret's swollen lips and the hard knot hidden within. But as soon as she touched Margaret's clitoris, Margaret put her hand out to stop her.

"Okay," Suzette thought to herself, "you just want to be fucked? Fine." Determined to keep going despite her exasperation, Suzette wriggled her thumb in next to her other fingers. Working slowly, she finally managed to shove her whole hand into Margaret. Suzette gritted her teeth and pumped away until Margaret came, screaming. Suzette let Margaret rest a moment with her hand inside. Then she instructed her: "Push." Margaret obliged, and Suzette's hand popped out of her vagina. Suzette stood up to look for the bathroom.

"Where are you going?" Margaret sleepily inquired, only mildly concerned. She felt quite content, and looked forward to fucking Suzette in a like manner.

"To wash my hands. I'm leaving. Mustn't be late for rehearsal, you know." Suzette scooped her clothes up in her left hand as she disappeared through the doorway. As though she had read Margaret's mind, Suzette stuck her head out of the bathroom long enough to say, "Maybe next time."

Margaret was aghast. She knew there would be no next time, but she didn't have a clue as to what had gone wrong. She lay on the pillows gasping for air. Suzette was counting on Margaret remaining in the bed for a few minutes, unable, perhaps, to stand. Margaret, for her part, was flat on her back. But it was mostly due to disbelief. No one had ever left her in the middle of sex before. Immediately afterwards, certainly, but even cads wanted their share first. Of course, with men, they frequently finished first. It was a rare man, she'd found, who could outlast her. Those that could she usually kept around for a while. No, it had been a long time since she'd had one of those.

Jennifer noticed that Suzette was shaking when the afternoon rehearsal began. Suzette gave an adequate performance, but Jennifer could tell that her heart wasn't there. During a five minute break, Jennifer cornered Suzette. "Care to talk about it?"

Suzette was too numb to be startled. "Talk about what?"

"Whatever happened with Margaret this afternoon." Jennifer smiled gently. "I saw you rehearsing together this morning. Something's obviously gone wrong since then."

"That's putting it mildly," Suzette sighed. Much as she wanted to confide in Jennifer, she was still cautious. "What sort of. . . thing. . . do you suppose happened?"

"Well. . ." Jennifer searched vainly for tactful words. "I suppose that Margaret took you home for lunch and got you into her bed. Then Margaret must have kicked you back out of it."

Suzette couldn't resist a wry smile. "Pretty close."

Jennifer impulsively reached out to Suzette, who had been trembling again. Suzette accepted the hug gratefully.

"How did you know?"

"Have dinner with me tonight, and I'll tell you." Jennifer's eyes twinkled as she turned toward the stage. "Break's over, I'm afraid!"

For the rest of the afternoon, Suzette managed to put the incident out of her mind. "I'll think about it later— maybe it would help to talk to Jennifer." She let her thoughts hide in the music. By the time rehearsal ended, she was breathing a little easier.

"Where would you like to go for dinner?" Suzette spoke first, letting Jennifer know that her dinner invitation had been accepted.

"How about the Olive Tree?"

Suzette winced, remembering her last visit there. Ordinarily it would have been a pleasant memory, but not today. "No— not there. Somewhere we can talk more privately."

"Then how about my place? We can pick up some Chinese food on the way." Jennifer winked. "That's as private as it gets."

"So you do that too? Take-out Chinese, that is." Suzette hesitated, frowning.

"Come on. You're safe with me. I promise."

Jennifer lived in a small, rather plain furnished apartment. The over-used furniture gave it a cozy, lived-in feeling that made Suzette relax in spite of herself. Jennifer bustled around finding plates and silverware, glasses and napkins. Finally they settled down to eat.

"Let's see. . . I believe I was just about to reveal to you my secret identity." Jennifer grinned. "I'm a lesbian."

Suzette managed to grin back at her. "I suspected as much, but you hide well. By the way, as if you didn't already know, so am I." Her faced darkened. "So tell me, how did you know about my little fling with Margaret?"

"I saw your rehearsal this morning. The electricity between the two of you was too strong for this average lesbian to miss. I wanted to say something to you then, but I felt I would be out of line. After all, I hardly know you. It was really none of my business. And when things have gone as far as that, it's too late to turn someone back. They have to turn themselves back."

"Then this afternoon you looked so shaken up, that I deduced the rest." Jennifer stabbed a shrimp with her chopsticks, taking revenge on Margaret in absentia.

Suzette laid her chopsticks down. "Very good, my dear Watson, except for one small detail. Margaret didn't kick me out. I left."

Jennifer nearly choked on a bean sprout. "You left?" She laughed, amazed. "Good for you! But why have you been depressed all afternoon? I would have celebrated!"

"Let's just say that it was an unpleasant experience." Suzette refused to say anything more about her afternoon. She moved on, instead, to the next dilemma. "I just don't know what I'm going to tell Cass."

"Who's Cass?" Jennifer was suddenly alert.

"My lover, of course." Suzette was mildly surprised.

"Oh."

Suddenly Suzette laughed. "This is crazy! I got so concerned with myself that I forgot— we've only just met! As lesbians, that is. I suppose by way of introduction I should tell you about Cass. She's a professional theater techie. We've been lovers for five years now. . . she'll kill me when I tell her what happened."

"Does this sort of. . . dalliance.. happen often?"

"Heavens no! This is the first time."

"Five years and you've never cheated on her before? That's a pretty good track record, if you ask me." Jennifer smiled encouragingly. "If you are really as devastated by all this as you seem, you won't have any problem convincing Cass that it was a fluke."

"You don't know Cass," Suzette moaned. "Life hasn't been all rosy at home lately anyway."

"Which is probably why this thing with Margaret got out of hand. Now maybe you two can settle down to normal." Jennifer pushed herself away from the table. "I'm stuffed."

"I'm getting there," Suzette lied, though her plate was still half full. In truth, she had lost her appetite. "I suppose I should be running along, if I'm going to call Cass tonight. I really don't want to, though."

"Don't put it off. It would only make things worse. Waiting would make you want to call even less, and Cass would probably be angrier knowing you had kept it from her." Jennifer put her hand comfortingly on Suzette's arm. "You can call from here, if you'd like. I'd be glad to give you moral support."

"No, this is something I have to do alone." With that, Suzette rose from the table. "I'll see you at rehearsal tomorrow. Good-night, and thanks. You've already given me the moral support I needed."

Arriving back at her apartment, Suzette began stalling for time. "Gertie, what am I going to do?" The cat eyed her sharply. "I know, I know. . . you think I should do the honorable thing, and confess. But what if Cass leaves me?" Gertie wound herself around

Suzette's legs, mewing sympathetically. Suzette poured herself a glass of sparkling water and went to the phone. "I suppose you're right, Gertie. I'll get over it eventually. But I don't want to! I don't want my life destroyed. The week before opening, too— I'm not only a slimy adulteress, but I have lousy timing as well!"

Suzette settled herself on the loveseat, equipped with water, phone, cat, and tissues. If she had had a seat belt, she would have fastened it. This conversation was going to be one long bumpy ride.

"Hello?" Cass' voice came cheerfully over the wire.

"Hello— Cass?"

"Hi, sweetie! How are you today?"

"Well, not very good, actually."

"What's wrong, darling?" Cass' voice took on a worried tone. "Has something happened?"

"Well, yes, actually."

"Darling, that's the second time in two sentences that you've said, 'well, actually.' Something *is* wrong. It's okay, you can tell me about it."

Hearing Cass in such a cheerful mood disarmed Suzette. She just couldn't make this woman unhappy. "I. . . had a really bad rehearsal," she lied. "I'm really worried about opening next week."

Cass clucked sympathetically. "I'm so sorry, love. But don't worry about next week. You always have a bad rehearsal before a good performance. You know your stuff— at least you needn't worry about your own performance."

Suzette sighed. She was disappointed in herself, but she continued in the same vein. "I guess you're right. It's really Margaret's performance I'm worried about." Suzette bit her lip. Cass didn't know just how true that statement was.

"You'd better get some rest tonight, darling. I know how that kind of rehearsal can wear you down. I need to get to sleep, myself. I'm behind schedule with the designs for our next production, so I'm going in early tomorrow. That means I probably won't make it up there this weekend." Cass cleared her throat. "I know you're going into Hell Week, but do you think you could come here this weekend? I'd really like to see you."

Suzette was relieved that she could say no. "I'm afraid not, Cass. I've got a sing-through on Saturday."

"Well, I guess I'll have to survive, then. I miss you already, though."

"But darling, I just saw you two days ago! And you'll be up next week for the opening, won't you?"

"I'm not sure I can make it. Like I said, I'm behind. I'll try my best, though." Cass sounded tired. "I think I'd better go. I'm really sleepy."

"All right. Good night, love. Thanks for talking to me." After Suzette had hung up the phone, she slammed her fist down on the coffee table.

"Chicken shit! Why didn't you tell her?" Anger swiftly turned to depression. Suzette curled up on the sofa with Gertie. She started to watch *The Women*, but even Crawford, Shearer and Russell combined couldn't cheer her. Defeated, she trudged upstairs to struggle vainly with sleep.

Chapter 11

Cass mulled over her conversation with Suzette while she finished her morning coffee. Last night it had seemed a normal occurrence, but in the fresh morning light Cass could see more clearly. Suzette had been acting strange. There was more going on than a bad rehearsal. Cass hadn't heard Suzette that distressed since her last cat had died. But if it had been Gertie, Suzette would have told her. That's not the kind of thing she would need to hide. What could have her so upset?

Cass' fertile imagination supplied her with lots of absurd possibilities. *Suzette has a crush on a man. No, too unlikely. How about: murder.* Cass chuckled to herself. *No way— she's not the type. Okay then, she's...* The thought that Suzette was cheating on her was too painful to consider. That fact should have warned Cass that it was the most likely possibility. Since she refused to consider it, she was ill prepared.

"Hello?" Cass queried.

"Hi— it's me." Suzette sounded tired after a night of tossing and turning.

Cass felt her stomach constrict. "What's up? You don't usually call at this hour."

"Well, about last night. I wasn't exactly telling the truth. I wasn't lying— I did have a bad rehearsal— but it was my own fault." Suzette gulped at her coffee before she continued. "I— I kind of had a little scene with Margaret."

That was it— a fight with Margaret. Cass sighed mentally. "I suppose it was bound to happen. I'm surprised that anyone can talk to Margaret and not fight with her. What happened?"

"I can't tell you." Suzette swallowed hard. She was starting to hate herself for being so cowardly, but then, she didn't want to hurt Cass either. Perhaps it was best not to say anything at all. Let her think they'd had a fight. After all, in a way, they had.

"Of course you can tell me. You've always been able to tell me everything." Cass sounded worried.

"Not this time."

"Come on, tell me!" Cass was becoming insistent.

"No." Suzette refused point-blank each time Cass pressed her for information. Finally Cass sighed mentally and gave up.

"Well, if you decide to tell me, you know where to find me. I've got to get to work."

"Good-bye, Cass. I— I love you." Suzette slowly hung up the phone. She would just keep Cass at bay until she forgot the whole thing. These two strange phone calls would be hard to live down, but she could do it. It would be better this way. Suzette didn't want to hurt Cass. Even more than that, she didn't want to lose Cass. It would take every ounce of Suzette's acting ability for a while, but she thought that she could do it. Resolutely, Suzette left for rehearsal.

Cass mulled over the morning's phone conversation on her way to work. Arriving at work she tried to put it out of her mind, but she couldn't. Something must be desperately wrong with Suzette, or she would have told Cass. Finally Cass decided to drive up after work and see Suzette. She was determined to find out what had happened.

Having arrived at a course of action, Cass felt better. She picked up her favorite drafting pencil almost eagerly and began to work.

At four o'clock Cass began to get impatient. "I'm going to knock off early today," she told her assistant. "I've got some things I need to get done this afternoon. See you tomorrow!"

Cass had a hard time keeping her car to the speed limit. She was anxious to arrive at Suzette's and find out what was wrong. At last she turned onto Windham. Cass could see Suzette's car parked behind the spacious old house, so she knew that she was home. With some trepidation she rang Suzette's doorbell.

Suzette had been dressing for dinner when the doorbell rang. Startled, she wrapped herself in a robe and went downstairs. *It must be Fred.* "I'll be right there!"

Opening the door, Suzette froze. There on her doorstep was Cass.

"Aren't you going to invite me in?" Cass asked as she leaned to kiss Suzette on the cheek. "I was worried about you, darling."

"Yes, of course, come in." Suzette recovered herself quickly. Closing the door behind them, Suzette put her arms around Cass. "What a pleasant surprise. And you needn't have worried," Suzette lied. "I was just about to go out and get some dinner. Would you like to come?"

Realizing that she had just driven a hundred miles on an empty stomach, Cass agreed. She followed Suzette up the stairs, seating herself on the bed while Suzette rummaged in drawers for clothes.

Suzette stalled for time, laying out her underclothes, her slacks, her blouse, even her shoes. For the second time since they had met, she felt uncomfortable undressing in front of Cass. The first time was the first night they had been together, and Suzette and

114

Cass had both been shy. The memory of that first night, of making love to Cass for the first time, filled Suzette with pain. Five years ago there was no way to know that she would eventually betray Cass. They had not even been able to foresee being together for five years, although it seemed as though they would be together forever. Sighing, Suzette kept her back to Cass as much as possible while she dressed. It was small comfort to not look at Cass.

Cass noticed that Suzette was avoiding her gaze. She knew that something was still wrong with Suzette, something she was hiding. Deciding to wait till after dinner before asking her again, Cass resigned herself to meaningless conversation.

Dinner was a sorry affair. The food tasted like cardboard to Suzette, but she forced it down. She didn't want Cass to suspect that she was upset, so she chatted about her day at rehearsal, relating amusing anecdotes. Cass noticed that Suzette ate almost reluctantly, and laughed too loudly at her own jokes. Something was most definitely wrong.

Arriving back at Suzette's apartment, they sat for a while on the sofa. Cass put her arms around Suzette, and although Suzette didn't push her away, Cass could feel the distance between them.

"Tell me what's wrong, darling. I won't give you a hard time, I promise. Haven't I always stood by you?" Cass spoke tenderly to Suzette.

"Yes," Suzette replied, almost inaudibly. She knew she wasn't doing a very good job of hiding her feelings. So much for her acting abilities. She knew she must look thoroughly miserable. She had to do something so that Cass would stop prying. "Cass, let's go upstairs. I think I just need to be close to you. Thanks for coming up here today."

"What else could I do? I'm worried about you. Maybe some quiet time together is what you need."

Suzette led the way upstairs. With each step, she wondered if Cass was right. It felt good, having someone who loved her enough to drive a hundred miles when she sounded unhappy. Maybe if she could just put Margaret out of her mind and concentrate on Cass. Suzette reached the top of the stairs and embraced Cass whole-heartedly for the first time since Cass' arrival.

"Mmm. . . that feels more like the Susie I know." Cass returned the hug gratefully. Suzette now needed to be mothered, pampered. Cass instinctively felt Suzette's needs change, and held her close. Mothering came naturally to Cass, although it wasn't apparent at first glance. She knew that she had come to Suzette for the very purpose of mothering her. Very gently she led Suzette to the bed. They lay down, Suzette softly enfolded in Cass' arms, her head on Cass' breasts. Cass knew that silence was the best way to nurture Suzette when she felt needy.

They lay quietly for a while. Suzette allowed herself the luxury of sinking into the warmth and comfort that Cass offered her. Gradually, though, Suzette began to realize the irony of taking comfort from the woman she had wronged. This idea expressed itself, not as words, but as a bitter-sweet pain. A single tear trickled down Suzette's cheek. When Cass tenderly wiped it away, her pain intensified. Suzette began to cry in earnest, silent tears streaming down her face. A great sadness filled her as Cass clasped her closer.

"Sh, darling, it's okay, it's okay," Cass crooned softly as she began to rock Suzette. Her voice, thick with worry, caused Suzette to cry harder. Soon her body heaved with sobs.

"Darling, what is it?" Cass asked with increasing concern. Her voice had lost its soothing croon.

Finally even sobbing wasn't enough to relieve Suzette's pain. In between sobs Suzette confessed.

Cass instantly stopped rocking. In disbelief she still held Suzette, her arms only cold comfort. Her mind was a complete blank, her body numb.

Slowly the shock began to wear off. She could again see Suzette lying in her arms, although she could not feel her. Cass felt as though she were under water, moving in slow motion. She seemed to see herself from above, from outside her body. Cass watched, detached, as her own arm lashed out, her open palm striking Suzette full across the face. Still in that eerie slow motion she saw Suzette's hand rise to her cheek as her head snapped sideways.

Suddenly time accelerated to its normal speed, then passed it. Suzette's crying stopped instantly. The slap had stunned her out of her hysterics. Neither woman had ever hit the other before. The unexpectedness of the blow added to Suzette's shock.

Cass jumped up from the bed. Almost before she knew what had happened, she was in her car headed for home.

By the time Cass arrived at home, the shock had worn off. She regretted leaving without getting an explanation. Rummaging in the kitchen, she came up with an old bottle of wine. Cass fortified herself with a glass of the wine, then went to call Suzette.

"Hello?" Suzette's voice was thick from crying.

"Hello, Suzette? This is Cass."

"Cass!" Suzette almost gasped. "I didn't think you would want to talk to me."

"I believe you owe me an explanation. Not to mention an apology," Cass said stiffly.

"You're right, I do. Oh, Cass, I'm so sorry. I've never been so sorry in my life. You've got to believe me." Suzette waited in vain for acknowledgement, then continued, wanting only to fill the awkward silence.

"I knew she was chasing me, but I thought I could handle it. I never imagined that I would succumb."

"But you couldn't resist her charms, is that it? How could you do that to me—to yourself? Sleep with that sleazeball!" Cass continued raving for a couple of minutes before Suzette could break in again.

"Oh, Cass, it was awful! But I've been so confused about us lately. . . I didn't know what to do."

Icy silence crackled over the line.

"It was awful—I suppose it served me right," Suzette continued. "That woman is a real sleazeball—a straight one, no less. I couldn't believe a woman could act that way. I wouldn't let her touch me. I walked out on her. Left her lying there, stewing in her own juice, so to speak. I couldn't face her again after that. I feel so dirty. Oh, Cass, I don't know how I'm going to finish this opera!"

At last Cass spoke. "I can't believe you're turning to me for help and comfort after you just finished cheating on me."

"I'm so sorry any of this happened. You've got to believe me. I never meant any of this to happen."

"You can't tell me she dragged you off and raped you. You obviously made some choices of your own here."

"I did, yes, I know I did. I was a total fool. You've got to believe that you are more important to me than anything else. . ."

"Then why did you do it? If you'd really cared about me, you wouldn't have gone off with that man-eating shark!"

"I don't know." Suzette tried unsuccessfully to stifle her sobs. "I felt like things were going badly with you...I was unhappy at home, I guess. . . oh, I don't know!"

Suzette's sobs were the last thing Cass heard as she gently placed the receiver back on the hook. She stared out the kitchen window into the night. She could barely make out the shadows that were her garden. Shades of black on black only added to her gloom. Dazed, Cass went through the motions of pouring herself a second glass of wine, then left it on the table, forgotten. She wandered through the house, looking at but not seeing all the trappings of their home. Their home, where they had been happy together only days earlier. Walking into their bedroom, Cass ran her fingers along the back of a chair, touched the bedspread, felt the hard wood of the dresser— all without seeing. Finally she closed her hand around a flat, round object on one bedside table. Grasping it tightly, she could almost feel it ticking, like a miniature heart in her hand. At last she uncurled her fingers and looked at the object, seeing it as though for the first time. It was the gold watch that Suzette had given her so recently. The newness of it, the love with which it had been given to her snapped Cass out of her trance. She fell on the bed and cried bitterly. All the hurt and anger, all the love she still felt for Suzette washed over her, pouring out in a hot shower. It was the first real relief she had received since she left MacAlister. After what seemed like hours her sobs slowed, finally stopping. Her body was completely drained, her emotions spent. Cass drifted quietly into a healing sleep.

Suzette didn't sleep a wink. The next morning she had to apply her makeup more heavily than usual to hide the dark circles left in the wake of her tearful evening and sleepless night. She thought about calling in sick. She knew Fred would understand and give her the day off. Everyone needs a mental health day occasionally. Finally Suzette decided that work was the best tonic. It would hopefully help her to regain her balance. Sighing, she dragged herself to the theater to sing.

Jennifer knew why Suzette was irritable at rehearsal, or at least, thought she did. She watched as Suzette forgot her music, forgot her words, forgot her staging. Maestro Kleinemann and Mr. Carlsen had both been irritated with Suzette all morning. That "thing" with Margaret must really have affected Suzette for it to throw off her performance. Jennifer knew that Suzette had built her career by being a real professional. Today, however, her professionalism had unraveled, leaving her vulnerability exposed. Jennifer decided to corner her at lunchtime to see if Suzette needed to talk.

Fred wondered what was wrong with Suzette. She was almost continuously making mistakes that she had never made before. Something was desperately wrong. Fred felt powerless during rehearsal. He had to keep order, so that the rest of the cast's time would not be wasted. Fred thought it might be easier to work without Suzette. Unfortunately her role was essential. Having the stage manager walk through Octavian's staging really wouldn't be satisfactory. Fred had seen Suzette have bad days and bad rehearsals before, but none as bad as this. Something must really be wrong this time. He would ask her about it at lunch.

Suzette could see the frost forming on Margaret's breath every time they were forced into contact. Unfortunately, with the intricate intertwining of their roles, that was far too often. Suzette decided that no one would notice, except Fred. If Margaret continued to be icy towards her, Margaret would simply turn in her usual bad performance. Suzette managed fairly successfully to ignore Margaret and her dagger stares. But she couldn't take her mind off of Cass. Suzette was convinced that her entire life was ruined. She hated herself for behaving as she had with Margaret. Alternately she hated herself for telling Cass instead of letting the secret die unknown. But then, she and Cass had never kept secrets before, and wouldn't a lie by omission eventually rot through their happiness?

Wouldn't the happiness become a mere facade, waiting to crumble completely? The questions, the doubts, the self-hating accusations continued to torment Suzette. She knew she was almost making a mockery of the rehearsal, but felt powerless to change it. Knowing that she was unintentionally sabotaging the rehearsal hurt Suzette's self-esteem even more. Her performance continued to go downhill along with her spirits.

Fred released them early for lunch. "Let's break now; I'll see you all at one. Suzette, could I speak with you a moment?" He wanted to catch her before they all could leave.

"Sure, Fred." Suzette dragged her feet up to the front of the stage as the others filtered out the back.

"Come on, I'm taking you to lunch. My car's out front," Fred said as he took Suzette by the arm and led her out through the house.

Jennifer watched them leave, disappointed. *Oh, well, I'll catch her later and find out what's going on.*

Fred and Suzette sat in silence as they drove. Fred stopped by the park where they had stopped many times since Suzette's arrival in MacAlister. They took their food to a far corner of the little park where they could talk.

"So. Tell me what's been going on. You are most definitely not yourself today." Fred spoke kindly, though his words seemed abrupt.

"Oh, Fred, it's Cass. I botched things pretty badly. I think she's going to leave me. I deserve it! I did it to myself. But I don't think I can face life without her. She's the woman I searched for years to find. She's sweet and tender, and strong and independent. She understands me: how I think, why I sing. She's always been so good to me, and I had to go and do this to her! If only I'd kept my mouth shut. If only Margaret had left me alone. . . if only I'd been strong enough to ignore her! But fool that I am, I was flattered; so then it was

121

too easy to get sucked into her clutches. But I can't even blame Margaret— it was all my own doing!"

So it was Margaret. I might have known, Fred thought to himself. "So what exactly happened?"

"Nothing! Everything! It was awful. She wanted me to be just like a man. She didn't want a woman. She didn't really want what a woman could give her. She wouldn't let me touch her body any where— she just wanted me to fuck her. So I did— with a vengeance. Then I walked out. She never touched me— not like that. I already felt too filthy to let her touch me. It was awful!"

"And you told Cass?"

"Of course! I couldn't not tell her. I tell her every-thing. If I hadn't told her, I wouldn't be able to see her again without thinking of it. Every time I touched her I would feel dirty. . . I would feel that my loving her was a lie. But it isn't! I love her so much, and now I wouldn't be surprised if she never spoke to me again. It's probably just as well. . . I think I must defile everything I come in contact with— I feel like a leper."

Fred wrapped his arms awkwardly around Su-zette. "No, you're not a leper. You're just a very human woman who craves affection, just like the rest of us. It must be very hard living away from Cass all the time. Maybe you need more time at home."

"I'll never be able to go home again. Not and have it be the same home it once was. I may never go back to that house at all. Cass will want it. She'd fight for it, I'm sure. We picked it out. . . bought it together. Maybe we can settle out of court. . ."

"What exactly did Cass say to you?"

"She didn't. . ." Suzette's calm veneer cracked, and she began to cry. "She drove up because she was worried about me. And then I couldn't cover it up— her tenderness towards me was too painful after what I'd done. So I told her. Then she slapped me! She's never struck me before, ever." Suzette paused to blow her nose. "She stormed out of my apartment. But then she called me later from home. I don't quite know why."

"Then how do you know she'll leave you? She'll be angry for a while, but she loves you, too, you know. I could tell when I saw you together. Don't you think she's strong enough to forgive you?"

"She's also strong enough to leave and never look back. I couldn't ask her to stay—I just couldn't. Not after all this." Suzette began to sob in earnest.

"Susie, I think you're being too hard on yourself. Get a grip! Even if she leaves you, you'll live through it. It's time to go back to rehearsal. Please try to pull yourself together. If you can't, perhaps you'd better take the afternoon off." Fred started to get up from the bench.

"I. . . I'll be all right." Suzette blew her nose, then dug in her purse for more tissue. "I need to be around people. I need to work to keep my mind off of all this. Thanks for listening to me babble. I just needed to get this out. You're the only person I've spoken to since I told Cass. Hopefully I'll be able to concentrate now that I've unloaded everything. I've got to put this whole mess out of my head for a while."

Fred helped Suzette rise heavily from the bench. "If you don't want to be alone tonight, you're welcome to crash at my place."

"Thanks, Fred. I just might."

Afternoon rehearsal went a little more smoothly. People noticed Suzette's puffy red eyes, but tactfully kept quiet. Margaret was among those who noticed. She gloated to herself. She felt that Suzette deserved any trouble she got. Leaving her in the middle of love-making! Such audacity!

Jennifer saw, too, that Suzette had been crying. She thought that Fred had been brow-beating Suzette over lunch. After rehearsal, she hurried up to Suzette.

"Would you like to have dinner with me? And talk?"

"No, thank you, dear. I've talked too much today already. Maybe tomorrow would be better. But thanks for asking. I appreciate your concern." Suzette gathered her composure around herself like a blanket, comforting, soothing herself. She didn't want to bare her soul again; not so soon.

Jennifer went home to fidget, wishing there was something she could do for the woman she respected so much. She was also a little angry. Suzette had taken her into her confidence before, and now, silence. She dialed Suzette's number, determined to know what new calamity had occurred. Finally, after a dozen rings, Jennifer gave up. She would find out when Suzette was ready to tell her.

The call from Jennifer wasn't the only call to Suzette's that went unanswered that evening. Every half hour, on the half-hour precisely, the lavender phone in her living room rang. Gertie sat and stared at it balefully, helpless to answer.

Cass stared angrily at her phone. Why wasn't Suzette at home? She must be with That Woman. The thought of Suzette seeking comfort in Margaret's arms inflamed her anger. And to think that she had tried to call to make up! Or to at least sort things out a little. She knew it would take her a long time to fully forgive Suzette, but when she first tried to call her, she had wanted to try. Hadn't she loved Susie through some unbearable times? What they had built over the course of five years was worth fighting for. Or was it? With each unanswered call, Cass became angrier and less inclined to work things out with Suzette. By the fifth call, she was ready to scream at Suzette, if she should answer. After the fifth call, Cass paced up and down the living room for a while, realizing that she had to get away. She had to get out of the house that reminded her so much of Suzette. Driving back to the school, she let herself into the theater building with her master key. Flicking on her office light, she stared out the window. The light streaming from her window made a solitary puddle on the sidewalk below. Finally she turned to her drafting table and picked up where she had left off that afternoon. Measuring lines and angles, figuring out how each set piece could work, all the precision of her drafting helped bring order to the chaos of her thoughts. She packed all thoughts of Suzette into little boxes and stored them in the back of her mind. Later, when those thoughts were not so fresh, when they had gathered a little dust in those boxes, she would take them out again and address them. Cass worked far into the night, until she could barely keep her eyes open to see the clean lines she had drawn. At last, having worn out her mind, Cass curled up on the old sofa she kept there. Sleep was mercifully quick.

Suzette shivered in spite of the warm fire Fred had built. He came out of his kitchen carrying steaming cups of cocoa, which she clasped gratefully in both hands. "I suppose I should call her tonight, to try and plead my case. But I dread it so! Somehow I can't believe she'll take me back. Calling is like asking for another slap in the face."

"You know her better than I do. I can't say whether it would be better to call or to leave her alone and let her sort it out herself. But it does seem as though you might want her to know that you care. If I were you I'd call."

"If you were me, you wouldn't have cheated on her. She's such a wonderful woman!"

"If I were you, I'd probably have cheated on her years ago. I'm not much of one for long-term fidelity."

"I find that hard to believe, coming from you, Fred. I think you just haven't found one man who was worth more to you than your career. And then, you would discover that you wouldn't have to give up your career, either." Suzette set her cocoa down in order to pull the afghan closer to her chin.

"You're probably right. But do you suppose I'll find one of those men anytime soon?"

"I don't know, Fred. I found a woman fitting that description, but now I've lost her. And I believe you only find one who's that special. The others will always have drawbacks. God, I'm stupid!"

They sat silently for a while, each in their own thoughts. Fred couldn't think of anything else to say. He could feel his friend's pain, as tangible to him as the heat from the fire. Fred felt completely unable to help her, so he let the silence gather around them like a buffer.

Suzette sat poring over and over what had happened. She would cling to her good memories of the past five years, then shatter them with more recent memory. Over and over she berated herself. When she could no longer stand it, she decided that action was the best cure. Rising from the sofa, she told Fred, "I think I'll call Cass now. That's the only way I'll know for sure what she's thinking."

Suzette slowly climbed the stairs to the guest room where she was staying. She wanted to make this call in private. Lying down on the bed, she quickly punched in those eleven familiar digits. Her breath and pulse quickened and she heard ringing on the other end of the line. One. . . two. . . three. . . twelve rings. Suzette laid the receiver gently back in its cradle. For the thousandth time in two days, she put her head down on her arms and wept.

Chapter 12

Friday morning Suzette dragged herself out of bed to discover that Fred had already made coffee.

"I thought you didn't know how to make coffee." Suzette teased.

"Don't tell anyone. It would ruin my image." Fred set a steaming mug in front of Suzette. "Besides, I thought you might need this right away."

"Thanks, Fred. You're right about that." Suzette sipped gratefully from the mug. "Now if you could just help me put my life back together."

"I'm no miracle worker, you know. Even if I do make good coffee. You have to work your own miracles. . . but first you need to put this whole mess out of your head. Concentrate on working. You know that your singing has carried you through a lot in the past. You also know that no one can ever rely on anyone but themselves. Since singing is a part of you, you can rely on it." Fred paused to drink his juice.

"I don't know, Fred." Suzette sighed. "This is the first time I've had to deal with this type of situation. I'm not sure I can do that anymore—not with something this big. A crisis of this size takes a lot of doing to forget. I think I've forgotten how to forget."

Fred resisted the temptation to smile at Suzette's last statement. Instead he changed tactics. "Well, then, what would you like to do to remedy this situation? If you can't forget it, maybe you should try to change it. Besides, you can't go back— only forward."

"What do you think I want? I want Cass back, of course! What else could I possibly want? But I'm just not worth it any more. She'll never want me back."

"That's what I thought it boiled down to. You want to be with Cass. I'll tell you now, as a friend, that the first thing you'll have to do is get rid of that defeatist attitude. Never say never! You are a worthwhile person, and you have to know that or you won't get her back. That is, assuming that you've lost her. You need to think of it as though you were courting her again. Be wonderful to her." Fred held up his hand to keep Suzette from protesting. "I'm not finished yet. You need to court her as though for the first time, only this time you have an advantage. You know all her weak spots, all the things she likes. Gardens. Moonlit walks— whatever. You know these things. But you have to use them to your advantage. Sell yourself like you've never sold yourself before."

Suzette let go of a deep breath. "This sounds worse than any audition I've ever sung! I don't know, Fred. I'll have to think about it." Crossing the kitchen for more coffee, she commented, "You know, I haven't stretched out or meditated in two days. Maybe that's part of my problem. How could I even begin to get my life in order if I'm off my schedule?"

Fred nodded his agreement. "That's right— do your usual thing. But you're welcome to stay over here if you need company."

"And advice! Thanks, Fred." Suzette put her mug down firmly. "Now I've got to go do my stretches. I'll have to hurry, though, or I'll be late for rehearsal."

"Don't forget your costume fitting," Fred smiled. "I thought you might be a little distracted yesterday, so I checked the call board for you."

"Anything else I need to know?"

"You're just singing all day, that's all. As usual! Costume fitting's at 10:00; oh, and dress parade tonight at 7:30. That should give us all enough time for dinner." Fred pushed his chair back and stood up. "I've got to run. I need to check in the scene shop to see how things are going— you know, make sure they'll be ready for Sunday's technical rehearsal. See you there! Just lock the door behind you."

"Thanks again, Fred. I'll think things over some more. Sometimes it takes an outside observer to give me a different perspective on things." Suzette stood and hugged Fred. "I'll see you there."

Suzette moaned as she stretched her muscles. Two days without her regular exercises were enough to make her body stiff. *I'll be sore tomorrow. Oh, well. That's what I get for neglecting my body.*

At last she finished, setting her clock for her meditations. Her time would be shorter than usual, since she hadn't planned on keeping up her entire morning routine, but it would be better than having nothing.

Sitting on the floor, Suzette had trouble collecting her thoughts. Stray ideas and questions ricocheted off the walls of her mind. *And this is what comes of neglecting my spirit. Chaos.*

With some difficulty she managed to calm her busy brain, filtering out all thought. After days of wailing to herself, the silence fell as a healing balm on her spirit. Suzette held the emptiness as long as she could. When her mind was again threatened by chaos, she calmly diverted her thoughts toward her body. She began gathering warmth into her limbs and torso. Her tired muscles began to loosen, relaxing into the warmth she had created. Finally Suzette felt that her calm would hold. She then allowed herself one question: *Why has Cass loved me for five years?*

The question hung suspended in her brain. Now the silence became fearful, ominous. What if there was no answer?

She needn't have worried. Soon images began to unwind for her. The first pictures were the most recent: the two of them playing in the park, having dinner at the Olive Tree, exploring Suzette's new apartment. Then she began to see older pictures, like a movie running backwards. There was Cass bringing Suzette iced tea with fresh mint after they had dug the garden because she knew Suzette disliked gardening. Then the two of them shopping for furniture for their new house: they had simultaneously fallen in love with an old lamp, crusty with age. After they had cleaned it, the lamp was beautiful. Its ornate bronze belly adorned a prominent place in their living room. *Who would get the lamp? — No! None of those thoughts!*

Making love in their new home for the first time, they made do without any furniture. Cass had been exploring the upstairs— looking into all the rooms and closets "just one more time." When Suzette joined her in the master bedroom, Cass caught her up in her arms. They had made love on the plush carpet, on the very spot where their bed would soon stand. Suzette couldn't help smiling as she remembered pleasing Cass. Cass, red hair flowing across the ivory carpet, back arched, breasts straining toward the high ceiling. . . she had shuddered and bucked so hard that Suzette could barely hang on. . . and afterwards, Cass had been so tender. . .

Time began to slip backwards more rapidly. Evenings at operas: Suzette watching the acting, Cass passing a critical eye over the sets, both of them enthralled by the music. Then Cass giving Suzette a tour of her *Tosca* set and sneaking a kiss inside the tower.

All the little things Suzette did for Cass, with Cass: working in the garden, bringing her simple daisies, dancing till all hours, waking her up with fresh coffee. Suzette watched her memories as they showed her their first months together. Getting to know Cass had been a joy. Cass herself seemed to take pleasure in Suzette's learning—yes, growing to love Cass had been easy. Romantic breakfasts in bed, making love at noon, hanging on the phone for hours when Suzette had to go out of town. . .

Suzette's reveries were broken by the beeping of her clock. Meditating by the clock was almost as bad as loving by one, she decided. Reluctantly she rose and showered. Allowing herself to think through some positive things she had had with Cass gave her hope. As she dressed, she decided to work hard on a positive outlook. Fred was right—if she didn't feel she had something to offer Cass, why should Cass want her? Yet Suzette wanted Cass to want her. She would just have to make herself desirable, irresistible. *Hold that thought*, she told herself as she hurried to the theater. *I'll just make it on time. . . I'll have to work on this later.*

"I'm glad I made it," Suzette whispered to Fred before they began. "I botched enough rehearsal time for everyone yesterday."

Fred just smiled. Suzette seemed much more herself this morning. The rest of the cast seemed to pick up Suzette's improved mood, and rehearsal went smoothly. Promptly at 10:00 a.m. Fred began rehearsing the big chorus scene in Act I, so Suzette slipped off to her costume fitting.

"Hi, Jill! Good morning, Katie." Suzette greeted the few costumers she had met. "I'm here for my fitting."

They greeted her and trundled her off to a dressing room, arms laden with rich fabrics. As Suzette pulled on Octavian's finery, she picked up her thoughts where she had left them earlier that morning. She more or less collected the memories she had found into a more concise package. Cass and she had loved each other for their warmth, their honesty, their mutual love of music, opera, theater in general... they held common interests, including a mutual respect for each other's profession. Each woman's strengths complemented the other's weaknesses.

That last thought gave Suzette hope. Perhaps Cass had enough strength of character to see beyond Suzette's moment of weakness. It was certainly worth investigating. Suzette was beginning to feel strong again, capable of attempting to restructure her life. It would never be quite the same again, but it could still be good. Now all she wanted was a plan of action—some glue with which to put the pieces back together.

Suzette finished pulling on her boots and went back into the costume shop. The costumers had done an excellent job. Only a couple of alterations were needed, and Suzette was quickly pinned and marked. As they finished the marking, Suzette found she had to forcibly keep her mind off of her last fitting. She was relieved to see that the next person to be fitted was not Margaret, but Jennifer.

"Hi, Suzette. How are you?" Jennifer consciously kept her voice light.

"Just fine, thanks."

"Care to have lunch today?"

"Sure. I'd like that." Suzette smiled. "Perhaps you can help me with some scheming. Is 11:30 okay?"

"I should be done here by then, and we don't rehearse again until afternoon. 11:30 it is."

"Fine. See you then."

Jennifer smiled to herself as Suzette left the costume shop. Now she would find out what was going on that had made Suzette's moods swing so dramatically over the last few days. It obviously concerned Margaret, but what was it? She would know soon enough. Jennifer's mind went back to her task at hand: the pile of petticoats that had been thrust into her arms.

Lunch was an interesting affair. Jennifer and Suzette found a quiet corner in a near-by diner to talk. As briefly as she could, Suzette brought Jennifer up to date.

"So you told Cass, and now you want to smooth things over. Where do I come in? I haven't even met Cass. . . and it seems like private luncheons with another woman would just add fuel to the fire, if the truth be known."

"As long as we behave ourselves, I don't see any problem. And, if everything works out as I'd like, I'm sure Cass will welcome you as a friend. Now, about your help. I need to think up a plan to woo Cass back. Help me think of some things to do!"

"You know her better than anyone. Make a list of things she likes— things you've done for her before. Better still, things you never quite got around to doing, but always wanted to."

"I suppose she probably won't let me near her for a while. . . she wouldn't answer the phone last night. But there's got to be a way around her defenses. I could write or send flowers. . . or both. . . that's pretty traditional. And gifts, of course, but it would have to be something unique— no box of chocolates would do it." Suzette propped her chin on her hand to help her think.

"I think a letter of apology would be the best step to take first. You've got to let her know that your indiscretion was a fluke. She needs to know that you've never wronged her until now, and won't do it again. Five years of fidelity has got to count for something." Jennifer turned her attention to her salad while Suzette continued.

"Okay, so a letter it is. Perhaps I could send the letter by messenger. Then I would know when it arrived, and it might help to convince her that I'm sincerely sorry."

Jennifer laid down her fork. "That's a good idea. You know, I could take it."

"No, we have the sing-through tomorrow, remember? I think it should go down as soon as possible. I'll find someone else. Someone Cass knows, at least a little." Suzette left it at that. Jennifer didn't need to know who she had in mind.

After the day's rehearsals were done, Suzette pulled Fred aside.

"Would you like to come over for dinner? I'd like to talk to you. We should have time before the dress parade tonight."

"Sure—but let's just send out for pizza. Delivery makes life so much easier."

"I couldn't agree more."

Soon they were both draped around Suzette's tiny living room. Suzette sat on the sofa, while Fred perched on a bar stool with his long legs neatly tucked beneath him. Fred covered the phone receiver with his hand as he asked, "The usual okay?"

Suzette smiled. "Of course, Fred."

The ordering done, he turned to Suzette. "So. What do you need to talk about? You're in much better spirits. I suspect you have something up your sleeve."

"I should hope so. I think I'm going to need every trick I can come up with to pull this together. I've been thinking all day about what you said. I've been working on my attitude— "

"I can tell."

"— and I've come up with a couple of crazy schemes. But I'll need your help. Tell me, are you going to be at the sing-through tomorrow?"

"I really hadn't decided, but I was thinking about it. It really is Maestro Kleinemann's department, but I should be there anyway. Why?"

Suzette leaned forward. "What would I have to do to talk you into going to Elmira tomorrow?"

"Now, wait a minute, Susie. Tell me the plan before we go any further with this conversation."

"Okay, okay. It's really very simple. I'll sit down tonight and write an apology, complete with promises, etc., etc. Then you carry it down and hand it to Cass in person. With flowers, of course. My part is really the most difficult— writing that letter." Suzette sighed.

"What's the catch? And what do I get out of it?"

"The only catch is that Cass may or may not willingly take that letter. I need you to plead my case, if necessary. Convince her to at least read it. And as for reward— you will gain my undying love, of course."

Fred chuckled. "You're starting to sound like the Susie I know. I thought I already had your undying love!"

"Well, that's true, I must admit. But still. . . I know you feel responsible for the sing-through, but I need you to do this. Please Fred— for me."

"You know me— I'm a real push-over. Especially when it comes to my divas and my friends. You're double trouble!" Fred sighed. "All right, I'll do it. But you owe me one."

"Thanks, Fred. I knew I could count on you." Suzette hopped up off the sofa. "We settled that just in time. Pizza's here! And this time it's on me."

Dress parade was the usual dull affair for the cast. Only the leads and a few sample chorus members were called for it. Fred loved it, however. While the singers were idling under the hot lights, he was able to examine the fruits of the staff's labors. Many chorus costumes had bits and pieces pulled from old costumes, rearranged into a new homogeneous whole. They were attired chiefly as servants. Most of them were in dark colors, with even the red coats of the footmen muted.

The Marschallin was stunning in a costume that satisfied even Margaret's heart's desires. Yards and yards of cobalt-blue velvet were draped over the large hoops, with giant loops and bows in a lighter shade for trim. The bodice, complete with built-in corset bones, fulfilled every exhibitionist fantasy Margaret had ever had. Under the bright lights, her snowy bosoms shone in all their glory.

Next to her stood Octavian. He and the Marschallin made a handsome pair, all in blues. But even next to the Marschallin's ebullient costume, Suzette caught Fred's eye. He took in every detail of her lithe body in the finely tailored outfit. *Susie makes a good-looking man. Too bad she's not,* Fred thought idly.

He took it back, though, when Gregory appeared, dressed as Baron Ochs. The Baron wore a rather garish red coat, the green and gold brocade of his waistcoat clashing loudly. But even in this outlandish costume, Fred admired Gregory's shapely limbs, clothed in hose and knickers. *It's just as well Susie's not a man—I might have missed out on Greg.*

The servants in Act II were done up in their finest black livery, creating a sharp contrast with Octavian's shining white and silver. Sophie shone in white also, with enough draping silver trim to out-dazzle even Octavian. When they walked out together in these outfits, even the costume designers let out a small gasp. For effect, they held first the lavish red velvet rose case, then the silver rose itself. They were dismissed from the stage quickly, for everyone was well pleased with their costumes.

Act III was done in various colors and shades of brown. The innkeeper wore a dark red waistcoat to make him stand out from the servants. Octavian's serving girl disguise was mostly reds with brown accents. The Baron appeared, garish as usual, in red and gold. Sophie and the Marschallin stood out from the rest in their blue and green costumes. In Act III the women only appear after the joke has been revealed, so their costumes had no need of blending with the browns and reds of the inn. Sophie now wore blue to match Octavian's usual male attire, while the Marschallin dressed strikingly in dark green. These colors had been chosen to show that Octavian and Sophie were meant to be together, while the Marschallin, old and tired, was alone once again.

Fred watched the colorful figures revolving, moving, kneeling, prancing on the stage as the costumers busily scribbled notes. The costume shop would be a flurry of activity for the next few days, but everything would go well. Very few costumes, if any, would have to be safety-pinned together for opening night. Fred smiled. He was proud of his staff. In turn his admiration of their craft spurred them to ever greater feats of the imagination. Together they maintained one of the most highly respected costume shops in the country.

When Katie declared that they had seen enough, Fred dismissed the cast. Tired but well pleased, he went home optimistic about the opera's opening. Nothing would have damped his spirits had he not remembered his mission for the following day. He decided that the only way to banish it from his thoughts was to turn in early. Once in bed, though, he couldn't sleep. He lay staring at the ceiling, wondering how Cass would receive him. Would she open her door to him? Would she slam it in his face?

Suzette, stripped of Octavian's finery, lay asking the same questions. At last they each drifted mercifully into sleep. The questions could only be answered— tomorrow.

Chapter 13

Cass awoke on the sofa, where she had spent the last couple of nights. She couldn't bear to sleep in their bed, the scene of many tender moments with Susie. Lying there, Cass stared at a beam of light that had escaped through the heavy drapes. Tiny dust particles sparkled in that beam, distracting her thoughts.

Tucking her favorite old quilt up under her arms, Cass sighed and pulled her thoughts together. She needed to figure out what to do about Susie. Her emotions were in turmoil. On the one hand, she hated Suzette for what she had done. She hated Suzette for being inconsiderate, for not thinking of her, for putting them both through so much pain. Yet Suzette's actions seemed in character somehow— something Suzette might do. Perhaps she should have expected something bad to happen eventually. It could have happened long ago, but hadn't. Cass felt that she had been lulled into a false sense of security by those five years of fidelity.

Then there were other factors. Did Suzette want out altogether? Was this act a rebellion against their relationship? Was Susie tired of her? But Suzette didn't seem to be trying to dump her. On the contrary, she seemed to be genuinely sorry. And their own lovemaking, just before this fling, had been wonderful. Then why had she cheated on her? Had Suzette really wanted to be with Margaret? Was she disappointed that that hadn't worked out, so she had come crawling back to Cass? Was she really sorry for what she had done, or was she just sorry for herself? But Suzette would have known that nothing could ever last between her and Margaret. From what she had told Cass, it was obvious that Margaret was only interested in short-term affairs. Margaret Byrd would never throw away her badge of respectability—her husband!

Looking back over the past weeks, Cass realized that Susie had seemed vaguely dissatisfied. She had been distant, moody. They had fought more than usual, which had made Cass uncomfortable, too. But it seemed like a passing discomfort—nothing serious. The last time she checked, she still loved Susie. But now her love seemed useless. Pain shot through Cass at the thought that Suzette might be discarding her. Would it hurt this much if she didn't still love Susie?

Tired of running in circles, Cass arose, showered, and headed for the garden. She couldn't seem to stop puzzling over Suzette, though. Finally, in her quest for a logical explanation for Suzette's behavior, she wondered if there wasn't one. What if Suzette's action had been totally illogical? Suzette was normally a very rational person, but it was still a definite possibility. Cass was stumped. What if it were true? How should she act? Should she— or could she— dump Suzette for this one irrational act?

Angrily Cass swung her hoe. How dare Suzette put her in this position! How dare she force a decision like this on Cass! Cass chopped weeds non-stop until her anger-fired shot of adrenaline was spent. Wearily Cass finished her weeding.

Trading her hoe and weed sack for a large basket, Cass began to harvest the ripe vegetables. At first she was able to concentrate on the task of gathering the fruits of her labors, but soon her thoughts wandered back to Suzette. Some of the care Cass gave to her garden began to extend toward Suzette. She started remembering times when she had nurtured Susie—times when Susie had needed her badly. The memories filled Cass with a pleasant warmth. She enjoyed mothering Suzette. It made her feel genuinely needed. It gave her a purpose in their relationship. What if Susie needed her now? She must be having a hard time, too. She probably needed Cass pretty badly right now— if she still loved her.

That last thought— *if she still loved her*— caused Cass to pause. That was something only Suzette could tell her. How could she figure anything out without hearing from Suzette? What if she decided on a plan of action that was entirely inappropriate? It was Suzette's turn to make the next move. Cass decided that her best course of action was to wait.

Having come to some sort of a decision, temporary as that might be, Cass felt relieved. Her garden work seemed to pass more quickly. Before she realized the time, the sun was high overhead and her stomach was growling. Selecting a few choice vegetables, she left the rest in the cool shed and went inside to fix lunch.

Fred left home just before noon, Suzette's letter safely tucked into the glovebox. He wanted to get this ordeal over quickly. Sometimes he amazed himself with the things he'd do for his friends.

Driving up to Cass and Suzette's house, Fred was impressed. The house itself exuded warmth and contentment. No wonder Suzette would be sorry to lose the place.

Fred stopped himself. No negative thinking! What a terrible attitude for Cupid. He sat for a moment, tapping Suzette's sealed letter against his palm. At last he could delay no longer and climbed out of his car, pulling after him the large bouquet of hot-house flowers Suzette had sent. On the porch he paused again before ringing the door bell, then pressed it once, gently.

An eternity passed in a moment while Fred waited. He was about to ring again, or perhaps retreat, when the door suddenly swung wide. There stood Cass, looking like the proverbial housewife, wiping her hands on a dishtowel.

"Fred?"

"Yes, it's me. Hello, Cass."

"What are you doing here? Is something wrong? Has something happened to Suzette?" All her old feelings of love came rushing in on Cass as she envisioned Suzette smashed between two cars, or lying in a hospital with every bone in her body broken.

"No, no, nothing's wrong," Fred assured her. He looked down at the flowers in his hands, shuffling his feet for a moment like a little kid. "I'm here as a sort of emissary. I wanted to talk to you for a few minutes, if you don't mind."

Realizing that they were still on the porch, Cass recovered herself and invited him into the house. She led the way to the kitchen in silence, Fred trailing quietly behind. Once they were both seated and supplied with coffee, Cass looked at Fred. "So what's your mission, or should I guess?"

"Well, my official business was to bring you this."

Cass took the slim envelope from Fred and turned it over in her hands. The familiar handwriting caused her heart to beat more painfully in her chest. Fred could see her already red-rimmed eyes begin to moisten. "I— I'd like to read this later— when I'm alone."

"I understand. But before I go, I wanted to tell you that Susie has been beating herself continuously ever since she started this mess. She misses you incredibly— I can tell. I knew her when she fell in love for the very first time. I can tell you that no matter how ardent she was in that first bright moment, no matter how intensely she has loved since, I have never seen her love anyone the way that she loves you. From hearing her talk, and seeing the two of you together, I know that her love for you is the kind that lasts."

"I don't know you very well, but from what I've seen, I believe that you love her the same way. If that is true, I know that you'll read whatever Susie's written, and take it to heart."

They both sat silently for a moment, then Cass spoke. "You know, to look at you, I never would have thought you could speak so eloquently. Thank you—I know you care about Susie, too. But I think you'd better go now." Cass showed Fred to the door.

"Thank you for listening to me ramble. I wouldn't have come down here if I didn't feel that every word of it was true." Fred held her hand for a moment before stepping off the porch.

"Yes, I know, Fred, I know. Thank you."

Cass closed the front door softly, then dropped face down on her make-shift bed to sob into her pillow again. It was some time before she could bring herself to open Suzette's letter. Finally she slit the thin envelope, drawing out one sheet of delicate paper. Cass' hand trembled as she unfolded it and began to read.

> Dear Cass,
>
> I'm so ashamed, and I hate what I've done so much that I can barely apologize. To say "I'm sorry" is an ineffective and meaningless phrase. And yet, it's true—I'm terribly sorry.
>
> If I could undo my actions, I would. I could never

repeat them, I swear. If another woman approached me now, I would run as fast as I could in the other direction.

I know that when someone cheats on her lover, chances are she's cheated before, or will again. I want you to know, in your heart, that this was the first and last. I learned my lesson the hard way. I hate what I've done to you. You are the dearest woman I know, and you mean more to me than anything— more, even, than my singing.

Please take me back. It may be asking too much for you to forgive, or even to forget, but I hope you're willing to try. Please! I love you more than I can say. Can I at least hope?

With All My Heart,
Susie

Cass cried a few more tears, but not for herself this time. These tears were for Suzette, for Cass now could feel Suzette's pain and fear. Cass still loved her. She had been badly wounded, but she had never stopped loving her. Suzette had written calmly and rationally in the beginning of her letter, it seemed, but Cass could see her softening near the end. Cass ran her finger over the words, "more valuable even than my singing." That must have been hard for Suzette to write.

Cass knew that Suzette had always placed her singing above all else. That statement alone was enough to break down any resistance Cass had left. She dried the last of her tears and drove into town to send a telegraph. It merely said, "Yes."

Fred had only missed the overture. Maestro Kleinemann was on his mettle today. The singers were also in good form, and seemed to be enjoying themselves. Fred thought he would never tire of hearing *Der Rosenkavalier,* if only he could hear this cast every time.

During the break between the first two acts, Fred told Suzette the details of his errand. They mulled over what had taken place, trying to guess at the results.

"You haven't told me much, except that she was polite to you, and listened. Maybe something you said will have helped."

"I did get the impression that she would read your letter— that she was in a mood to be receptive. I think your best bet lies there."

Suzette gulped her vending-machine coffee and crumpled the cup. "I certainly hope so."

Fred glanced at his watch. "We'd better be getting back, or the maestro will have my head! It's a good thing we're not doing *Salome,* or I'd end up as Fred the Baptist."

Fred's feeble attempt at humor succeeded in prompting a smile from Suzette. It wasn't easy, but she felt that she could survive until she heard from Cass— maybe.

Act II went smoothly enough to suit even the maestro. The chorus had ample time to sit and listen, and they were obviously enjoying the music. After Octavian and Sophie's touching scene together, the rest of the cast couldn't help but applaud. Maestro Kleinemann, himself, was too pleased to reprimand the chorus for breaking silence. No one noticed the stage manager tapping Fred on the shoulder, beckoning him off-stage.

"I thought this might be important, but I didn't want to stop the rehearsal," the stage manager whispered.

"Thanks, Barb. You did the right thing." Fred felt a shiver of anticipation as he took the crisp envelope in his hand. "I'll give this to Suzette during the next act break."

Fred wandered out to take a seat in the house and the stage manager returned to her post in the wings. Fred slipped the telegram into his jacket pocket, dropping the jacket over the chair beside him. He had trouble concentrating on the music now. He was distracted, knowing what was now in his care. Perhaps the telegram signaled the advent of their reconciliation. Fred hoped so. Then they could all get down to work with clear minds. That was important, with the opening less than a week away.

At last the act drew to a close, and Fred hurried backstage. He managed to grab Suzette out from under Jennifer's inquisitive nose.

"Suzette, I've got to talk to you. In private." Fred tossed a meaningful glance at Jennifer.

Suzette just nodded, following him outside. Jennifer stood gaping in their wake.

When Fred pulled open the outside door, a cold blast hit them full in the face. They found a spot where they were sheltered from the wind before Fred turned to face Suzette.

"Well, Fred, what is it?" Suzette pulled her scarf more snugly about her neck. "Make it quick—I shouldn't be out in this!"

"I don't know whether this is good or bad— they say no news is good news. Since I wasn't sure, I almost waited for rehearsal to end. I confess, my curiosity got the best of me."

By this time, Suzette's impatience as well as her curiosity had been piqued. "So what's going on?"

"Before I tell you, I want to caution you to remain calm. If the news is bad, you've got to put it out of your mind till after rehearsal." With that, Fred drew out the telegram.

"Oh!" Suzette grabbed the telegram, then stopped. Perhaps she shouldn't open it. Then suddenly, decisively, she ripped it open. One glance was all she needed. Suzette was stunned. To have all her questions, all her torment solved in one small word overwhelmed her. Then slowly she began to laugh. Her low chuckle quickly grew to almost hysterical laughter, so great was her relief. Tears streamed down her face as she laughed. Fred was so relieved in his turn that he, too, began to laugh. At last their laughter subsided and they were able to calm down. Life suddenly seemed more normal to Suzette than it had in weeks, though many times more precious. When they finally made it back inside, they were late for Act III. Maestro Kleinemann soon forgave Suzette, however. Her face beaming, Suzette's voice soared. Octavian enjoyed his tricks and frolicking more than ever. Suzette, as indeed everyone, had sung well in the first two-thirds of the rehearsal. Now, however, she sparkled as never before.

Fred beamed, too, as he watched her. He felt like a benevolent father. *I knew it— I just knew it would be all right. And listen to her sing! That's what love can do for you.*

When rehearsal was over at last, Maestro Kleinemann complimented them all. "Keep this up, and our opening will be breath-taking! I hope your staging goes as well." He climbed down from his podium amidst moans from the singers. He shook hands with his concertmistress as the official end to their last sing-through.

Suzette could hardly wait to get home and call Cass. Yet it was still with some trepidation that she depressed the numbered buttons. What should she say? Should she talk to her as if nothing had happened? But that was impossible. Maybe she should send a note. But Cass had answered her letter right away. Shouldn't she do the same?

Suzette heard the other receiver picked up mid-ring. There was a slight pause that seemed interminable before she heard Cass' familiar voice.

"Hello?"

"Hello, Cass? It's me— Suzette."

"Hello." Cass, too, seemed at a loss for words.

"I just called to tell you that I got your telegram." Suzette hesitated. "And that I love you."

Cass' reply was almost inaudible. "I love you, too."

Suzette felt as though she were treading on eggshells. "May I. . . see you this week?"

Then Cass laughed, breaking the tension that had stretched the phone wires taut. "Of course! I wouldn't miss opening night for anything, silly woman!"

"Good, good!" Suzette grinned. Now they were back on familiar ground. "The sing-through went very well today. We should have a good opening. How's your latest project coming?"

"I've finished the basic designs for the *Flute* set. I just have some details to work out now."

"Which could take forever! I remember those 'details.' It must be just little things, like, how do all the pieces fit together, and what keeps the set from falling down!" Suzette couldn't stop grinning. She had seen Cass labor for weeks over similar "details."

"Well, yes," Cass confessed, "plus figuring out the special effects. Appearing and disappearing food and wine, people flying in and out, the trials of fire and water. . . you know, little things like that. Shouldn't be too difficult."

"I can hardly wait to see it! You'll have to give me the backstage tour of this one for sure."

"Certainly. And I'd like a backstage tour of your opera— I haven't been on the stage at the Cosmo. You know me. I love to snoop around in other people's rigging."

Suzette just chuckled. She knew it was true, in more ways than one. "So when do you think you could make it up here? You know I won't be able to get away this week of all weeks. We're dark on Thursday, but that's my pre-show rest and relaxation day. I'd love to have you up here to help me relax, though, if you can get away."

"I don't know, Susie. It depends on how much I get done this week. I'll be taking Friday off for sure, so I'll at least be up Thursday night. If I can get a little bit ahead, I'll come Wednesday. I'll let you know."

"Okay. Just be sure to call and tell me so I can get my chores out of the way. Better call during the morning hours. There's no telling when I'll get out of dress rehearsals. Tomorrow we could be there all night— it's the first tech."

"I know how that goes. My heart goes out to your poor stage manager tomorrow."

Suzette stifled a yawn. "I'd better get some sleep. May I call you tomorrow?"

"Of course. I would like that." Cass felt the formality returning to their conversation. She sighed. "It's been awfully good, just talking to you like old times. I hope we can keep it this way for a while. I. . . I need to heal some more."

"I'll do anything I can to help you. . . I hope you know that. But when you want to talk about it, maybe we should. It would be good to clear the air more."

"You're right. I'm just not ready to talk about it yet. Maybe when I see you I'll feel better. Besides, I'd like to talk about it in person."

"My only request is that we not spend a lot of energy on it the day of opening or the day before. I need to be selfish on those two days. But before that, or after, would be okay. You name it."

Cass made a mental note of Suzette's request. "That seems reasonable enough. I know those two days always affect your opening performance. If I can't come up early, we'll just call a truce for those two days."

"Thanks, Cass. You've always been so thoughtful." Suzette smiled. "I love you, sweetie," she said warmly.

"I love you, too, Susie. Oh, and Susie," Cass continued, "I've missed you."

Suzette felt a too-familiar tear beginning to sting her eye. "I've missed you, too. Maybe we could take a vacation soon—just us. Fred was of the opinion that we need more time together. Maybe he's right. Maybe being apart so much has hurt us."

"That reminds me—tell Fred thanks for me. His timing today was impeccable. I'd been thinking all morning, and, well, he showed up at just the right time to remind me that I really do love you. It helped, I think."

Suzette sent up a quick *thanks, God* before replying. "I'll be sure to tell him. He'll be glad to hear it."

"Well, I'll let you get off the phone. I know you've got a long day ahead."

"Good night, sweetie. Sleep well."

"I will, thanks. Good night, love."

After she hung up the phone, Suzette felt suddenly drained. A lot had happened in one day. Resisting the temptation to simply fall asleep on the sofa, Suzette scooped Gertie up in her arms and climbed the stairs. Sleep came quickly for the first time in many long nights. Gertie sensed her mama's contentment. The cat curled up in the crook of Suzette's legs and sighed happily as she, too, settled down for a peaceful night.

Chapter 14

Sunday came much too early. The excitement of the previous day left Suzette feeling slightly hungover. She dragged herself through the morning, going through her usual routines. The only break in routine was a quick call to Cass, but she was so sleepy that she cut the conversation short. She seemed physically unable to say anything of importance whatsoever. Finally she gave up and took a nap after lunch. Suzette knew that the evening rehearsal would be very taxing. It would take all her energy and concentration to keep her cool. Technical rehearsals are notorious for their tediousness and length.

After her nap, Suzette still felt groggy. She decided to go for a walk to get her blood moving again. Once she had stepped outside, she pulled her cloak more closely about her. A chill breeze quickly brought a red tinge to her nose and cheeks.

"Mmm...feels like snow weather," Suzette said to the overcast sky.

"We'll have a hard frost tonight, at least."

Suzette turned in surprise. "Hello, Irene. I didn't expect anyone to be out in this weather."

"Neither did I." Irene smiled warmly and patted Suzette's arm. "I always take a walk at this hour. But why are you out? You must take care of your throat."

Suzette returned her smile, amused at the older woman's maternal behavior. "I'm just trying to wake up before rehearsal. With the help of this wind, I think I'm succeeding. Tell me, would you and Joseph like to see the opera? We open Friday, and I'd be more than happy to arrange for tickets."

Irene was obviously flattered. She had taken a liking to Suzette. "I'd love to! But I'll have to check with Joseph," she added, "He has trouble sitting still for long. You know how it is."

"I understand. But I do hope you can come, if you'd like. Joseph can always step out for a moment if he feels like it. And I would feel that I had begun to repay you for all you've done for me."

"But we haven't done a thing," Irene protested, though she was obviously pleased. Then she admitted, "I would like to see you perform, though, dear. It's been a long time since we've been to the opera."

"Then consider it done. Just let me know soon which night you would like to attend."

"Thank you, dear. Now I'd best be off. I've walked my bit. I'll speak to Joseph tonight and let you know."

"I need to get moving, too. I have rehearsal soon. Good-bye, Irene. Say hello to Joseph for me." Suzette took her leave and headed for her apartment as Irene left for the main house.

Once inside, Suzette fed the cat and gathered up her things. She stopped at her favorite diner for a bite to eat, then headed for the theater.

Suzette was a few minutes early. Seeing the flurry of activity onstage, she skirted the area and found a seat in the house. A moment later Fred appeared from the shadows and took a seat next to her.

"Well?" Fred asked.

"Well, what?"

"What happened with Cass? I know you must have called her last night."

Suzette smiled. "We made up, mostly. It was awkward and tense at first, but then we just talked—you know, like we always do. It was such a relief, just to speak with her."

"You've certainly moved fast. I'm surprised to see this situation wrapped up so quickly."

"I don't think it's entirely 'wrapped up,' as you say. I think we've got a lot of work to do on our relationship. Not new things, particularly—more like old problems that we weren't aware of before this. So I feel a need to tread lightly for a while. I'd like to do some nice things for Cass. On Friday I called a friend of mine in New York City who's working on one of my surprises. I hope she can finish it by Friday—I know one week isn't much time."

Fred grinned at her. Now you've got my curiosity going. Can't you at least tell *me* what it is?" When Suzette shook her head, Fred teased, "Oh, come on, you can give me a hint at least. Just one tiny hint!"

Finally Suzette gave in to his childish begging. "Oh, all right—but just one hint. It has something to do with the opera."

"This opera?"

Suzette nodded, but refused to give him any further information. When he continued to pester her, she simply said, "One clue. That's all you get, for now, anyway."

At last Fred gave up and tried a different tactic. "So what else do you have up your sleeve? You must have more than this one secret."

"You're right, I do. The next item on my agenda is this." Suzette dropped an unsealed envelope into Fred's lap.

Fred slid the embossed card out of the envelope. "It's an invitation to the ball on opening night."

"Yes, but not just any invitation. I'm not inviting Cass to be my guest. I'm asking her to be my date."

"Your date!" Fred almost dropped the card. "You do realize what that means?"

"Of course— but don't you think you ought to start rehearsal? We're going to be here late as it is."

"You're right, as usual." Fred rose from his chair. "But I hope you've given this 'date' a lot of thought."

"I have Fred, believe me." Suzette also rose. "I'll explain later. Let's go!"

Rehearsal was, as predicted, dismally slow. Stage hands scurried backstage, and the stagemanager seemed to be everywhere at once. Onstage the action moved in fits and starts. Minor problems, such as sticky doors and windows, only slowed the rehearsal's progress. Larger difficulties stopped the action for minutes at a time, and major catastrophes caused longer breaks. Fortunately there weren't many major catastrophes.

Most of the delays occurred during the large scene shifts. Between Acts I and II, moving furniture was easy but time-consuming. Flying the walls out was a bit more difficult. The walls for Act II had large decorative sconces that caught on the Act I walls high above the stage. No amount of shaking or swinging the huge structures would free them. It took three stage-hands perched precariously on top of tall ladders to disentangle the mess. After the excitement was over, the stagemanager merely sighed and added one more note to her long fix-it list.

During the Act II to Act III shift, the crew forgot to unlock one of the many trap doors in the floor. In the midst of the scene between Baron Ochs and Octavian as the serving girl, there came a loud pounding on the floor directly beneath the Baron's feet while he was singing. Gregory jumped as though he had seen a real ghost. His reaction sent the rest of the cast into a fit of laughter, releasing some of the tension of the evening. A stagehand went running downstairs to fix the problem. Then they backed up a few measures and tried again. This time when the "ghost" rose through the floor, the trap door creaked loudly. The scene continued, but the stagemanager made another note. It looked like the traps would have to be oiled every night, just in case. The trap doors were more trouble for the singers than for the stage crew, however. The men who were to pop through the floor at various times had to practice balancing on their tiny staircases while gently opening and closing the doors above them. Suzette was seldom near the trap doors when they were opened, but Gregory was often directly in front of them. Once when he turned around, he narrowly missed falling into a hole that had opened up behind him. Fred let them blunder through the tricky portion of the act, knowing he had scheduled extra time the next day for it. Finally the joke in the plot was revealed and the cast gratefully began the end of the opera.

Everyone had been fidgety all evening. It was difficult for certain singers to deal with a rehearsal in which they were not the center of attention. People wandered off to get drinks or for no reason at all, occasionally missing entrances. When a few chorus members missed entrances the rehearsal could proceed without them. Unfortunately Margaret Byrd was ten minutes late for her entrance in Act III, which held up everyone. Some chorus members and a few leads, such as Suzette and Gregory, maintained their professionalism. Suzette, at least, wanted to set a good example for the rest of the cast, as well as keep their respect.

Out in the house, Fred sat with the lighting and costume designers, trying to keep from pulling out his hair. He knew that by the very next night his dedicated crew would have everything running smoothly. They were planning to stay late to practice the scene shifts.

Still his heart stopped when he saw two large fire-places collide, or a chorus member narrowly escaping decapitation by a flying wall. At last it was all over, and the cast gratefully made a mass exodus.

Fred managed to catch Suzette before she escaped. "You can't leave me on pins and needles all night. I know it's late, but let's go for coffee."

"Fred, what's more important? You knowing right now, this instant, what's on my mind, or you having a well-rested, happy singer tomorrow?" Suzette tried unsuccessfully to keep from sounding cross.

Fred sighed. "You're right— again, damn it. But could we at least have lunch tomorrow?"

Suzette smiled. Fred could still be as petulant as ever. "Of course. Is 11:30 all right? I'm planning on taking it easy in the morning!"

"Sounds fine. I'll pick you up— that'll simplify things."

"Thanks, Fred. Now, good-night. And please don't worry."

"Good-night," Fred said, not promising anything. He went home expecting to toss and turn half the night. In truth, the rehearsal had worn him out, and he was soon snoring.

Cass went to work extra early Monday morning. She wanted to get her work done so that she could surprise Suzette on Wednesday. Now that Cass knew where things stood with Suzette, she was anxious to see her.

Around mid-morning Cass decided to take a coffee break and call Suzette.

"Good morning!"

"Mmm? Oh, hi."

"'Oh, hi?' Is that all you can say for yourself? Better wake up, sleepy-head."

Suzette moaned. "What time is it, anyway?"

"It's late! I let you sleep till ten."

"Ten o'clock? It's definitely time to get up. Listen, can I call you back after I've had a cup of coffee? You know how I am in the morning."

"Of course, darling. I'm at work."

Cass smiled to herself as she went back to work. Suzette hadn't changed a bit.

Half an hour later, Suzette called back. "I'm feeling more human now, love. Hope I wasn't too gruff when you called."

"No more than usual. I'm used to it, though." Cass pushed her chair back and propped up her feet. "It's a good thing you decided to keep me around. Who else would put up with all your little quirks?"

"No one, I guess," Suzette replied. "I would just have to spend the rest of my days in the old maids' home."

"But sweetheart, there's no such thing. There's only the old dykes' home, and you'd be out of place. Lesbian widows only need apply."

"Well, I'd better behave, then, so you'll stick around. I know when I've got a good thing. I may have forgotten temporarily, but darling, I swear I've re-gained my sanity."

"Suzette?"

"Yes, dear?"

"Let's not talk about that right now, okay?"

"Okay. I'm sorry, I wasn't trying to put a damper on our morning."

"It's okay. Just forget it." Cass took a large swallow of coffee to keep herself from getting upset.

"You should have been here last night." Suzette decided that the best tactic was to change the subject. "Greg Loft and I were doing the beginning of Act III. I was sitting on the bed while he was singing and strutting about in the Baron's usual pompous man-ner, when there was a terrific banging under Greg's feet. I'd swear he jumped five feet off the floor! If he could simulate that same terror every night, he'd bring down the house."

Suzette had chosen the right maneuver. She had set them off on a round of old backstage tales, telling one amusing anecdote after another. Both of them knew all their stories by heart, but they never failed to make each other laugh. Eventually all the morning's strain was gone.

Suzette wiped tears of laughter from her eyes. "Much as I hate it, I'd better go. Fred will be here soon to pick me up, and I haven't even had a shower!"

"And I've got to get back to work. I'll talk to you later. Have a good rehearsal tonight—it's your first dress, isn't it?"

"Yes, but just costumes—We don't have to wear full make-up until tomorrow. It will be my first time in public with a cod-piece, though."

That thought was enough to send Cass into yet another fit of giggles. "I haven't laughed this much in ever so long! It feels wonderful to laugh with you again. Too bad you have to go. I guess we'd better hang up or we'll never get off the phone."

"You're right. Good-bye, sweetheart. I love you."

"I love you too. 'Bye." Cass hung up the phone and sat a moment, enjoying the warm glow left from the phone call. Then she picked out a drafting pencil and went back to work.

Fred parked on the street and walked up the gravel drive to Suzette's door. He heard an unintelligible shout in response to his knock that he assumed meant come in. Sure enough, the door was open and Suzette was nowhere to be seen. Fred settled himself on the sofa to wait.

Suzette popped her head down the stairs in her robe to say, "I'll be ready in a minute," then disappeared again. Ten minutes later she reappeared, fully clothed. "So where to?"

"I thought we'd head for that little café downtown that you like so much."

"Perfect. Let's go."

Minutes later they were seated at a small green table, perusing menus. After they had ordered, Fred got down to the business at hand.

"Now. Tell me about this date for the Grand Ball. Whatever possessed you to do such a thing?"

"I've been thinking about Cass, and what I could do to make her realize what a large part of my life she is. I want her to know just how important she is. And it's not just that, Fred. It all goes back to the dichotomy in which I live. On the one hand, I'm a lesbian. I live in a beautiful home with my lover— all very idyllic, really. Then, on the other hand, I'm a singer. Worse, I'm a well-known opera singer. Those are the two sides to my life, and ne'er the twain have met. The problem is that each of those sides affects the other, whether anyone's aware of it or not. My vocation affects my life with Cass, which is fine. In fact, she fell in love with my opera-singer side. In addition, my being a lesbian affects how I look at the world, how I approach my music, how I feel when I'm singing. . . you know. It can alternately be my inspiration and my downfall. And yet most of the people I work with and most of my audiences don't know why I do the things I do. It's true that the essence of opera is to create an illusion. But people also perceive the opera, in part, according to their previous knowledge about the performers. Take Octavian, for instance. The audience knows full well that I'm a woman. Yet when I go out on stage dressed as Octavian, they will choose to see me as a young man."

Suzette could not keep her serious face at her next thought, and broke into a grin. "So if they knew I was a lesbian, *Der Rosenkavalier* would be more of a lesbian opera than you envisioned with your harebrained scheme. This opera could be more sexually radical than you thought!"

Fred chuckled with her. "I see what you mean. But would you really want that?"

"It would be amusing, but actually, I don't think things would happen that way. Lesbians have always had a problem with invisibility. I think that habit of ignoring the existence of lesbians would enable the homophobes in my audience to continue to see Octavian as a man. More liberal people might get a chuckle out of the idea, just as we did. And, presumptuous as it is for me to say this, perhaps a young lesbian or two would see me and know that not all lesbians are downwardly-mobile."

Suzette paused as their lunch arrived. After the waitress had gone, Fred asked, "But if you're suddenly becoming concerned about other lesbians, don't you think you'll be condemned by the 'community' as a whole?"

"First of all, I've always been concerned about other lesbians, just not publicly. If anything, they should trash me for keeping to my closet for all these years. If they want to condemn me for being famous, I'm sorry. I won't be doing this as a 'movement' thing. I have always followed my own heart, and opera, strange as this may seem to some lesbians, is a large part of my very being. You know me. I couldn't stop singing classical music any sooner than I could cut off my own hand. Now here is my heart dredging up old trouble. I've always been disturbed by my two-faced life, and now I have new troubles on top of that. Troubles I've created myself. Somehow, though, I have a feeling that they're interconnected."

"What do you mean, interconnected? I'm not sure I follow you," Fred said as Suzette took a bite of salad. "I understand all too well the discomfort of leading a double life. I also realize that, in some ways, the two

159

sides to our lives affect each other. But what has all this got to do with Cass?"

"I think I was vaguely discontent before, not because I was unhappy with Cass, but because of my double life. It got stirred up when you tried to turn *Der Rosenkavalier* into a lesbian opera. So what did I do? I tried to get rid of my discontent somehow. But since I thought that I was unhappy with Cass, my reaction was directed at her. Obviously, cheating on my lover was not the right thing to do. I know that two wrongs don't make a right. I only wish I'd figured this out sooner!"

"I see," Fred commented. "But I'm still not sure I've figured out quite what the Grand Ball has to do with your problems."

"It's time for some positive action. First of all, taking Cass to the ball would let her know how important she is to me. She would understand all the implications of such an act. Besides, I think she would enjoy it. I know I'll have a better time dancing with her than some male patron of the arts! Secondly, as you know, it would be my grand coming-out in the opera world. My debut at the Cosmo would also be my debut as an 'out' lesbian. Add the two together, and hopefully my inner peace will return. That should help me to work better and to hold up my end of my relationship with Cass. I most fervently hope so, at least!"

"Whew!" Fred was amazed. "I hope this all turns out well. Your hopes are awfully high. But I must say, I don't see any real flaw in your reasoning. My only question is, what if the operatic community reacts badly? You could lose contracts, friends, family— what about your career?"

"First of all, Cass is my family. The rest of my family has known for years about my lesbianism. They won't be pleased, but we'll still be on speaking terms at least. My friends either know already or are fairly liberal. I'm certain to lose some friends, and others won't associate with me publicly, but I'll get over it, and so will they."

"Now, about my career. I'll move to Europe if I have to—I will continue to sing. I can't stop. You know that. I feel that I will find some way to continue my career. I do not feel that this will happen, though. I think the opera world will continue to ignore my lesbianism just as it always has. Homophobes are notorious for their ability to deny your very existence, even with evidence right in front of them. From now on, I will simply include Cass in any public activity that she would like. When I'm near home, as now, she can go to all the parties with me that she wants. I think she'll like that— she's always felt left out. She also hears second-hand about the people I work with. Well now she's going to meet them, through me. Not through some other channels and not as my 'friend.' She's my partner, my lover, my spouse. And I'm not going to act as though I were ashamed of that anymore."

By now Suzette's feathers were quite ruffled. Fred did his best to soothe her. "Calm down, now, no one here's attacking you. I've met Cass, you know, and I like her quite a bit. I think any of your colleagues who are the least bit human will like her too. You certainly have every right to bring Cass to opera parties. There's really no use, though, in railing against homophobia. You'll only feel worse in the long run. I think your best course is the one you've mapped out already."

Suzette knew that Fred was trying to placate her. She felt better for having spewed out her distress and anger, so she let herself be soothed. After she felt calm again, she interrupted.

"Fred, I'm okay now, you can stop babying me. Now you know, though, why I'm sending that invitation to Cass. Which reminds me—I would like to drop it off at the post office after lunch."

"No problem. It's not far from here."

The two friends finished their lunch in comfortable silence, interspersed with an occasional remark about the upcoming rehearsal, or a comment on the last one.

"My treat today," Suzette said as she picked up the tab. As Fred began to object, she held up her hand to silence him. "No— it's the least I can do for someone with as wonderful a pair of ears as you have. Besides, you can catch it next time!"

Fred drove Suzette to the post office, keeping the car and its heater running while she went inside. Once she was back in the car, Fred commented on the chill weather.

"Yes, it is nippy. I thought it would snow yesterday. Too bad it didn't," Suzette said.

"I rather think it's a good thing. You wouldn't want Cass driving up here in the snow, now would you?"

"I see your point."

"By the way, when is she driving up?" Fred inquired.

"I'm not sure— probably Thursday. I should know for sure by tomorrow," Suzette replied.

"Got anything special planned? Let me know if you need some help."

"No, I don't think I'll need any help for what I have planned. I never have before."

Fred noticed Suzette's serious tone and glanced at her. Then, catching the twinkle in her eye, he laughed.

"You sly thing— planning a close encounter of the romantic kind, eh? Sounds like the most helpful thing I can do is stay out of your way!"

"Seriously though, Fred, you may be able to help me on Friday night, before the ball. But you're right, I've already chosen the welcoming committee— me."

"Here's your house. I'll see you tonight. Thanks again for lunch." Fred reached over and gave Suzette a quick hug. She returned it, then got out of the car.

"See you later, Fred. And thanks for everything."

Suzette spent the afternoon watching *Mildred Pierce*. Deciding finally that fiction was drearier than life, she went to the theater ready to work.

Suzette was shown to a private dressing room. Julie had brought her costumes and left her to herself, telling her to call down the hall if she needed help.

Since the cast wasn't wearing full make-up, Suzette knew that she could be dressed quickly. The other women would take much longer to dress in their many layers of petticoats. Suzette took her time, enjoying the rich fabrics of her costume. When she was dressed, Suzette strutted up and down the hallway, feeling the weight of her clothing. She had worn the boots and sword in other rehearsals, so she had become accustomed to them. The sword felt different, though, more appropriate when worn with the rest of the costume. Suzette felt its swing and practiced pulling it out of its scabbard. At last she felt comfortable, and decided to show off her costume. She sauntered over and burst into the chorus women's dressing room. At first they pretended to be flustered and embarrassed, then flirtatious at the presence of a "male." After the women had clowned around for a few minutes, they began to tease her good-naturedly.

"She makes an awfully cute boy," one woman winked.

"Look, she's even got her own equipment," another remarked, nodding her head in the direction of Suzette's crotch. "Planning on using it anytime soon?"

"Why? Do you want a demonstration?" Suzette retorted, effectively silencing at least one heckler.

Gradually the chorus women went back to their own dressing, and Suzette left them. She had received the attention she wanted in her new costume.

Rehearsal was relatively uneventful. Suzette quickly assimilated her costume into her movements.

The other women had more difficulty maneuvering in their hoop skirts, but most of them had worn similar costumes on previous occasions. The evening was mostly work for Suzette, her pre-rehearsal antics being her only playing for the evening. When the opera was over, Suzette gratefully removed her heavy costume. She hurried home to her cat and the inviting comfort of her bed.

Chapter 15

Tuesday went by in a flurry of activity. Fred spent the day making sure of last-minute preparations for the opera. Cass worked feverishly to finish her project. And Suzette went shopping. She bought gifts for Cass, groceries for a romantic evening at home, and a new formal for Friday night.

That night, Suzette went to the theater early and settled into her dressing room. She had fun experimenting with her make-up, working to make herself look like a young man. The powdered period-style wig did much to aid the illusion. After she had finished her facial creation and dressed, she ran into Jennifer Doyle in the restroom.

"Powdered wig notwithstanding, I'd always be able to tell you're a woman," Jennifer noted, glancing at Suzette's still-apparent breasts.

"The men in those days must have been terribly femme," Suzette countered.

Jennifer grinned, then commented, "You do look incredibly butch in those boots, even if the rest of the outfit is fit for a flaming queen."

"I'm not sure whether that's a cut or a compliment! Maybe I could loan this to one of my more flamboyant friends." Suzette glanced at the clock. "I have to go. It's almost time to start."

"See you in Act II!" Jennifer was still grinning to herself as the door swung shut behind Suzette.

Suzette had decided not to confide in Jennifer her plans for opening night. She wanted Jennifer to have every opportunity of disassociating herself from the whole mess if she wanted. Suzette felt the need to keep interactions with Jennifer brief, like the one they had just had. In a way, she felt selfish. This was to be her coming-out, and she wanted to keep it to herself.

Suzette put all such thoughts aside and concentrated on the opera. The rehearsal went fairly well. Suzette was still enjoying the effects of her costume. It helped her to move and feel more like Octavian. She got into her character more than ever that night, carefully storing the new sensations in her brain for future use. Suzette was enjoying herself and concentrating so hard that she was surprised when the opera ended. It seemed to end as soon as it began.

The next morning, Cass went to work early. She figured she had about two hours' work left before she could leave town. She rechecked all her drawings and calculations, working diligently to create an accurate cost estimate and finish the supply list for her new set design. She knew that she could take the time to do the job right. The overtime she had put in for three days in a row allowed her that luxury. Two hours and several cups of coffee later, as she had predicted, Cass was on her way back home. Reaching the bottom of their driveway, she stopped to check their mailbox. There, in the midst of a handful of bills and junk mail, was the invitation from Suzette.

Cass was delighted to find the heavy cream-colored envelope addressed in Suzette's hand. She forced herself to drive up to the house, park the car and go inside before opening it. Every second she delayed increased her anticipation. Finally she dropped into a chair at the kitchen table and slit the envelope open with a handy butter knife. Cass ran her fingers lightly over the face of the embossed card.

You Are Cordially Invited to Attend
The Grand Ball
to be held in the Grand Ballroom
following the Opening Performance
of The Cosmopolitan Opera Company's
Der Rosenkavalier.

Cass' hand trembled and she almost dropped the card. She and Suzette had agreed years earlier that they would not attend public social functions together. Yet here was an invitation to the social event of the year. Cass let her hand drop to the table in amazement. Then she caught a glimpse of the scribbles inside the card. Opening it, she read Suzette's note.

My Darling Cass,
Would you do me the honor of accompanying me to the Grand Ball? I think we would both have a good time. Just think— ballroom dancing, champagne, a fancy buffet— and you could meet some of my other friends and colleagues.
I probably don't have to remind you that there will probably be people at the ball with whom you have worked or may work in the future. Don't hesitate to say no if you want, but if you turn me down because of the exposure, please tell me. I want to know. I don't want to think that you simply didn't want to go with me.
Please respond, s'il te plaît. I anxiously await your reply.
With All My Love,
Suzette

Cass was astonished. Of course she would go! This was a momentous occasion. Cass was glad she was heading up to MacAlister early. Such an invitation deserved a reply in person. She packed hurriedly, deciding to shop for a new ball gown there. It would take too long to shop before leaving home. Cass made a few quick stops in town, then headed north.

Suzette slept late, then puttered around doing chores. She wanted everything to be just right for Cass' arrival. Irene loaned Suzette a vacuum cleaner, broom and mop, and she cleaned diligently. Suzette was vacuuming her bedroom when there was a knock behind her on the open doorframe.

"The door was open downstairs so I just came on in."

Suzette whirled around in alarm, which quickly turned to delight.

"Cass!" Suzette leapt toward the door. She threw her arms around her lover's neck, oblivious to the bundles in Cass' arms. "I didn't expect you till tomorrow."

"Darling, careful," Cass laughed, "you're smashing your flowers." She soon forgot flowers, luggage and all, however, as she melted into Suzette's kiss.

Suzette and Cass pulled out of the kiss slowly. They stared into each other's eyes, scarcely able to believe they were together again. It seemed eons since they had last been loving and intimate. Suzette tried to pull Cass down onto the bed, but Cass' burdens were in the way. Bags, boxes and flowers tumbled to the floor before the two women realized what was happening. They both stared in dismay at the mess, momentarily disarmed. Then Suzette began to laugh.

"We've been mooning about like teenagers in an old movie musical," she gasped. Her laughter was contagious, and soon both women were helplessly hysterical. They collapsed on the bed amidst the debris and laughed till their sides ached. Gradually their laughter dissipated into the slightest of hiccoughs, then disappeared altogether.

"Darling, I'm so glad you're here," Suzette said.

"And I'm so glad to be here," Cass whispered back. This time nothing hindered their embrace.

After a time, Cass pulled away from Suzette. "I can't wait, love. You've got to see what I brought you."

"Wait." Suzette delayed her momentarily. "I've got something for you, too."

"It's just a little something," Cass remarked. "I wanted you to know that I do still love you, in spite of everything. You're still you, after all. Maybe more so than ever." Cass handed Suzette a long, flat box.

Suzette slid the ribbon off the box and opened it. Inside lay a pair of long white gloves, yellowed slightly with age. There were beads sewn in an elaborate pattern on the side of each glove.

"These are the gloves I wore in *Die Fledermaus*," Suzette exclaimed, holding them up to the light, the beads sparkling. "How ever did you get them?"

"The woman who runs props owed me a favor. I paid for their replacement, of course. But it is a wonder I found them. Digging through boxes and boxes of gloves took a while." Cass grinned. "I spent so much time staring at you during that opera. You were dazzling. I could have recognized those gloves anywhere."

"Thanks for the compliment. You were too incredibly beautiful a woman to be lurking backstage. I'm surprised I never missed an entrance, I was so busy watching you." Suzette poked Cass playfully. "I loved flirting onstage because I knew you were watching."

"How did you know?" Cass protested. You were busy onstage with Eisenstein."

"Ah, but I, ze Hungarian princess, see all." Suzette let a giggle escape. "I peeked at you whenever I could. You were pretty obvious, darling."

"Well, you were awfully blatant yourself. How many opera divas send flowers to the set designer/stage manager?"

"Oh, a few, I'm sure." Suzette feigned innocence.

"Every night of the run? You can't fool me, Miss Etoile." Cass laughed. "Now show me my present."

"Okay, but first you have to RSVP."

"RSVP? Oh, the ball! How could I forget? I'm sorry, darling, I got carried away with everything else. Of course I'm going. I'm positively thrilled that you asked me. That is, if you're sure—if the invitation still stands."

"Of course, love. I'll explain all about it over lunch. But now you have to open your gift." Suzette handed over the small package. "It's a dreadfully selfish present, I must say."

Cass opened the box. Inside lay an ivory fan, with an old-fashioned dance card attached. "It's beautiful—but why do you say it's selfish?"

Suzette reached into the box and turned the dance card over. "That's why," she said simply. Cass looked and saw Suzette's name written next to every dance. "You wicked woman! You want to monopolize me for the entire evening."

"You've got it." Suzette smiled. "But you'll notice I'm down in pencil. You can always erase me."

"No, darling, I could never erase you. Your name, however, is another matter. I may find someone else to dance with—Fred, for example. You may have to wait until we get home to monopolize my time." Cass winked at Suzette playfully.

Suzette laughed again, pulling Cass back down on the bed. "Maybe we should practice our dance steps now."

"May I cut in?" Cass stopped her. "I hate to end our dance so soon, but I'm rather hungry."

"Lunch!" Suzette came quickly back to reality. "I'm

sorry, love, I didn't realize it was so late."

"That's okay, sweetie." Cass gave her a quick kiss on the cheek. "How about lunch at the Olive Tree?"

"Mmm...brings back delicious memories. I'll be ready in five minutes."

Half an hour later the two women climbed into Suzette's tiny car. As they pulled out of the driveway, Suzette slid her hand affectionately along Cass' thigh.

"I'm so glad you're here. I've missed you dreadfully." Suzette removed her hand just long enough to shift gears, then replaced it. "I would like to talk to you about us, and about me. We need to clean up some issues before we'll feel completely together again."

Cass nodded. "I know. I don't want to talk, but I agree that we need to. Maybe we could make a pact not to create a scene in public."

"I promise." Suzette patted her leg comfortingly. "I'm not sure a truce is necessary, though. I think some of the things I want to say will please you, and some will surprise you. I only hope that all of it makes sense."

"Thanks for promising anyway. I have enough trouble dealing with this in private." Cass squeezed Suzette's hand.

"I would just like to explain some things to clear the air. Then maybe we can start again fresh."

"I would like very much to have a clean slate with you, Susie. I'm not sure it's at all possible. I do think that if we both try, we can overcome this crisis. We have to use the bad times to bond us closer— we can't let one problem drive us apart." Cass paused, then continued. "If we were to break up over one offense, even as heinous as infidelity, then I question the strength our love had in the first place."

"Many people break up over less." Suzette had winced at the word "heinous," but did not comment. She wanted to object to the strength of the word, but in a way she felt she had earned it. Instead, she merely said, "We're here. Time for lunch!"

Restaurant rush hour was over, so Suzette and Cass were seated immediately. The Olive Tree's menu at lunch was more conventional than their dinner menu. Nevertheless, the two women were indecisive. Finally Suzette tossed her menu onto the table.

"I give up. I'll just have a spinach salad. And hot tea."

"I think I'd like the avocado cheeseburger. It sounds more filling," Cass said as she laid her menu lightly on top of Suzette's. "Make my tea iced, please."

"Wait until you see their spinach salad," Suzette said after the waitress had gone. "You just think a burger's more filling!"

Cass and Suzette lapsed into silence as the waitress brought their drinks. When they were alone again, Suzette plunged in head first.

"I want to tell you why I decided to 'come out' by bringing you to the Grand Ball. My explanation may be strange and convoluted, but I'll try to make sense. My desire to 'come out' is connected with my recent infidelity, in a way. You remember Fred's crazy scheme back when we first started this opera— he wanted Octavian as an actual woman. Remember how much the idea of a lesbian operatic role disturbed me? Yet it excited me at the same time. I haven't been quite the same since. I thought that the issue was closed when I decided to veto the costume and staging changes, but it wasn't. For the last month I've had a gnawing sense that something in my life wasn't quite right. Somehow that unsettled feeling became associated with you, and our relationship. I know you sensed my unease."

Cass nodded, remembering strained conversations, but didn't interrupt.

"Discontent seems to feed on itself. My unhappiness kept growing until finally I had to do something.

I must have been looking for something to make me feel good again. I obviously didn't find that something—quite the opposite. I almost totally destroyed the happiness I had found with you. But I was operating under the assumption that my problem was related to you. Now I believe it was not. I want you to know that I'm not trying to excuse what I did. I'm just trying to understand, and hopefully help you understand as well, why I cheated on you. If you believe that what I'm trying to tell you is true, maybe it will make it easier to trust me again, eventually. I'm convinced that my whole difficulty stemmed from my split life. I love you, and I want to do everything with you—as much as, or even more than, when we first fell in love. That's why I want you for my date to the Grand Ball."

"I see. And you've considered the ramifications?" Cass' tone was quiet and serious. This new information would take time to digest.

"Yes, I have." Suzette repeated the explanations she had given to Fred the day before.

"Suzette," Cass finally said, "I need some time alone to think over what you've said. I'd like to pick up my car at the apartment and leave you for a few hours. I want to shop for a few things, and I think that would give me the space I need."

"Anything you say, love. Let me pay the check and we'll be on our way."

When they reached the apartment, Cass followed Suzette inside. Closing the door, Cass slipped her arms around Suzette's waist.

"Can I have a hug before I go?" Cass asked.

Suzette's reply was to wrap her arms around Cass. They held each other for several minutes.

"Please come back to me," Suzette whispered. "Don't disappear from my life."

"I won't, darling. I'm just going away for a couple of hours—I promise." Cass pulled Suzette even more tightly to her. "I'm not sure what's going to happen, Susie. Sometimes I feel as though I'm sitting on a volcano, and sometimes I feel totally empty. The emptiness is as bad as the volcano— I feel numb, then, like the calm before a storm."

"I know, sweetheart. I've been expecting— I don't know what. Something, some...retaliation. You've been so wonderful for the last week or so. I don't deserve your good treatment."

"Well, if you want me to beat you, forget it. Berating you would be exactly what you want. If I got mad it would make you happy. You would feel absolved somehow."

Suzette was surprised at Cass' small outburst. "Is that what you think? That I want you to verbally abuse me to make me feel duly punished? Maybe you think I haven't been punishing myself enough."

"How could you possibly?" Cass tore herself from Suzette, pacing halfway across the room. "How could you ever hope to match the level of pain and humiliation you've given me? You don't know how I've suffered since you cheated on me. Real despair is something I doubt you've ever felt. Have you ever felt unloved and unwanted? Have you, Susan? Have you?" Cass spun on her heel to face Suzette. "You may have felt dirty after screwing around with that woman. You should have. But you can't begin to know how slimy I felt knowing you had touched me, too. You— you're sick! Diseased! How could you possibly purge yourself of that? I've been damaged, and you want to redeem yourself? I was burned because I trusted you, and you want me to trust you now? I feel like a lamb led to slaughter. And here you've tried to be so 'rational' about the whole mess. Well it isn't rational! Slapping your lover in the face by sleeping with another woman— a straight one at that— is not the act of a thinking woman! Then today you made me sit there

174

and listen to your lame excuses. I don't understand how you could do such a thing! How could you? I hate it! And I hate you!"

Cass had been shouting, but by the end of her tirade she was weeping. She had flung all the invectives she could muster. Now that her ammunition was depleted, Cass reluctantly let Suzette pull her down onto the sofa. Cass sobbed heavily on Suzette's breast. Suzette rocked her like a baby, tenderly running her hand through Cass' hair. Suzette longed to whisper soothing words to her but feared she might make the situation worse.

Gradually Cass' sobs subsided. After blowing her nose and drying her eyes, she smiled sheepishly.

"I guess I needed to rampage," Cass said quietly.

"I'm not surprised. Do you feel better now— about us?"

"Yes...yes I do," Cass replied, her eyes sparkling now, "but I still need to go shopping!"

"Do you think I could go with you now?" Suzette asked, glad to see that Cass' mood had been improved by her outburst.

"I could probably take you along, except that I want to surprise you."

"Well, in that case, have a good time! Only...when do I get the surprise?" Suzette prodded. "I won't be able to wait long."

"I'm afraid you're in for a hard week, then, dear. You can't see it until Friday."

"I have a little surprise for you on Friday, too." Suzette winked mysteriously. "Two can play this game."

"Oh, this surprise isn't for you— it's for me. You, however, will be surprised." Cass grinned at her lover. "I'm in the mood to splurge on myself."

"Then you'd better get moving. Those moods don't seem to last long for you." Suzette gave her a gentle nudge as though to push Cass toward the door.

"I should be home by dinnertime, if not sooner. You know how easy I am to please." Cass gave Suzette a quick kiss, picked up her wraps and purse and left.

When Cass returned, empty-handed, Suzette had just risen from a nap.

"Didn't you buy anything?" Suzette asked, yawning. "You were certainly gone long enough."

"Of course I did, silly woman. I left it at the store to be picked up Friday. You didn't think I would bring it back here where you would be tempted to peek, did you?" Cass laughed. "Now pull yourself together, sleepy-head. We need to get some dinner before your rehearsal."

The two women had a quiet dinner, then went to the theater. There Suzette introduced Cass to Barb, the stagemanager.

"I'd like to look around for a few minutes, if you don't mind. I promise not to get in the way," Cass told Barb. "Being in this business myself, I know what it's like to keep tripping over people."

"That's fine," Barb replied. "Help yourself. I won't have time to give you the guided tour. Just be sure to grab a seat in the house before we start. That's when we get really crazy backstage, you know."

With that, Barb put on her headset and began barking commands to her crew. Cass knew that she had been dismissed. She began to explore. Cass knew how to become invisible backstage, so she was able to hunt out all the nooks and crannies without getting in anyone's way. She inspected everything from the basement, complete with storage and the staircases leading to the trap doors, to the grid high above the stage. When she had gotten as close to the grid as the elevators could take her, she slipped off her heels and scaled the iron ladder bolted to the wall.

"If Suzette could see me up here, she'd kill me. I should have worn jeans— I just knew it," Cass murmured to herself as she climbed. When she reached the top, she stood, shoes in hand, gazing down at the tiny people and scenery below. Then she began to mentally inspect the system of pulleys that allowed scenery to be raised and lowered.

"Plenty of room. That always makes it easier to devise an efficient system," Cass said aloud. "I wish mine were this nice. We're always so cramped." She took another look down at the stage, then turned and made her way back down. Another quick glance at the rigging from stage level, and it was time to find a seat. As she turned to make her way toward the house, maneuvering carefully past the hoop-skirted women, a gentleman in blue winked at her. Two seconds later she realized that the "gentleman" was Suzette. Cass waved, then went out and took a seat.

Cass loved to watch Suzette on stage, loved to hear her sing. She sat enjoying the sights and sounds. Cass would sometimes watch an opera from a technical point of view. She would puzzle over how a structure was built or how an effect was created. Today, however, she had the eyes and ears of a child as she allowed herself to be dazzled by the spectacle.

The only shadow on her evening was seeing Suzette bending lovingly over Margaret. Jealously, Cass dug her nails into the arms of her chair till the tête-a-tête had passed. She was consoled by the fact that it was just an illusion— and the fact that Margaret was obviously stone-cold throughout that scene.

After the opera ended, Cass sat and gossiped with Fred about the opera. Suzette finally appeared, clean-faced and dressed in her usual garb.

"I see you two are as thick as thieves tonight. What's up?" Suzette asked.

"Nothing, just chattering." Cass smiled at Suzette. "Would you like to go for coffee with Fred, or are you too tired?"

"I'm not too tired, but I would like to go home. I had something more fun than coffee in mind." Suzette winked at Fred. "I'm sure Fred won't mind."

"No, no, I don't mind." Fred sighed melodramatically. "You two run along. I'll be fine, going home all alone to my big empty house."

"Suzette," Cass said gently, "I'd like to go out with Fred. We have all day tomorrow to stay home together. You can even sleep late."

"Well..." Suzette showed signs of yielding.

"Besides," Cass added, "you need to get used to staying out late. I want to dance all night Friday."

"You know I can't refuse you anything, darling. Of course we can go." Suzette grinned. "See, Fred, she wraps me around her little finger."

The three friends drove to an all-night café. They chattered and laughed over coffee and pie, sticking to safe subjects. All aspects of opera were open for discussion, as well as Suzette and Fred's college antics. Cass loved hearing their stories about the good old days, but none of them wanted to talk about more recent events. Finally all three were exhausted. Even Fred agreed that it was time to go home.

"Good-night, Fred. Drive safely," Suzette said as they parted at the door.

"You, too. Till Friday. Don't get too rambunctious tomorrow," Fred cautioned. " You need your rest!"

"Okay."

"I'll keep her under control. I promise," Cass said, grinning. "She'll be under my thumb all day."

"I'll bet," Fred retorted as he climbed into his car. "Good-night, gang."

Suzette and Cass drove home and undressed in silence. Both were weary after the long day. Slipping into the wide bed next to Suzette, Cass sighed happily.

"It feels so good to be next to you. I've been lonely lately, sleeping by myself."

"I know what you mean. I've missed the touch of your skin." Suzette snuggled close to Cass, who folded her arms around her. Each woman breathed the scent of the other, content to lie close. The bedclothes were soon heavy with warmth, weighted with night. Gertie joined them, curling up at their feet. The bed seemed to be a safe place, an oasis. Soon the three, Cass, Suzette, and Gertie, drifted gently into sleep.

Chapter 16

When Cass woke, Suzette was still sleeping soundly. Looking around, Cass decided that the light coming through the windows seemed muffled somehow. She sat up to investigate, discovering much to her delight that it had begun snowing. She almost woke Suzette, but changed her mind. Cass wanted to keep the snow to herself for a little while.

Slipping out of bed, Cass made her way quietly down the stairs to the kitchen. She went through into the bathroom, gazing out the window at the snow falling amongst the trees. The ground was already lightly dusted with the fine powdery white. Even as Cass watched, the ground was becoming less and less visible. Soon trees, house and all would be covered.

Cass backtracked into the kitchen. Peering into the refrigerator, she found a few lonely food items. *That's just like Suzette. She obviously never eats here.* Seeing that the food was all fresh, Cass realized Suzette was planning on cooking that day. Pulling out eggs, bacon and cheese, Cass began rummaging around for utensils. She managed to unearth a skillet and spatula, and quickly turned out a couple of decent omelets. Suzette's coffeemaker held a prominent position on one counter, and Cass soon had coffee as well. Plates and cups were easy to find, but no trays were to be seen. Cass lined the plates up on one arm, grabbed the mugs with the other and charged bravely up the stairs.

"It's snowing!" she announced triumphantly when she reached the top. "Sit up, woman, I brought breakfast." Cass set the dishes on the dresser as Suzette struggled to open her eyes and sit up.

"Morning," Suzette mumbled. "Coffee?"

"Yes, darling, I brought coffee." Cass handed her a mug and sat beside her on the bed. "Drink a few sips and I'll hand you your omelet."

The two women ate in style, balancing plates on knees and watching the snow filter down.

"I can't believe it's snowing," Suzette exclaimed as soon as she was fully awake.

"Beautiful," was all that Cass could add.

Food, then plates, rapidly disappeared. As soon as her hands were empty and idle, Cass turned to Suzette.

"I see you're finally awake. So what are your plans for the day?"

"Pure recreation," Suzette replied. "I intend to just play around all day."

"Like this?" Cass inquired, leaning over to kiss and caress Suzette.

"Yes, something like that." Suzette returned the kiss with a longer one.

"Mmm... your skin feels so good," Cass murmured as she slid down to lie next to her lover.

"I've missed yours," Suzette whispered in agreement. "I've longed for the taste of you," she said, running her wet lips along Cass' shoulder. Suzette nibbled slowly toward Cass' neck, then ran her tongue along a sensitive strip by the collarbone. From the hollow of the neck, Suzette followed a familiar winding path down and around the sensuous curves of her lover's body.

With each successive lick or nip Cass became more vocal. Her original murmurs gradually became moans as delicious sensations flooded her body. Her every nerve was soon electric with pleasure. Suzette was searing Cass' flesh with tongue flicks of lightning.

After torturously slow meanderings, Suzette finally reached Cass' most deeply hidden, delectable spot. Cass gave a low cry and stiffened, trembling. She hung suspended as though on the brink of a high cliff. Just when Cass felt she could no longer bear it, she felt herself flung over the edge into the sea, where the tide soon carried her to gentler waves.

"Thank you, love," Cass whispered, pulling Suzette up by her side. "I needed you so badly."

Suzette merely nodded and lay still. Cass held her close, wanting to be quiet for a few minutes. Gradually Cass felt her strength returning.

"Now it's your turn," Cass said, turning to kiss Suzette full on the mouth, running her tongue along the most tender places. Suzette broke the seal at last, gasping.

Cass proceeded to tease Suzette unmercifully. She used the knowledge of years, touching every nerve ending Suzette had. Alternately wet or dry, cold or hot, Cass' fingers and tongue burned into Suzette's flesh, leaving her permanent, though invisible, mark.

Suzette quickly scaled the peak Cass had so recently left, clawing the air as though to climb faster. On reaching the top, she filled her powerful lungs, proclaiming her triumph with clarion sounds as she crashed back to the earth. Shattered, she lay silent.

Suzette and Cass spent the day enjoying each other's company in and out of bed. They had a romantic candlelight dinner "à la Suzette," then cuddled on the lavender loveseat to watch old Garbo movies. When it came time to go to sleep, Suzette was quite worn out.

"I'd better behave myself tomorrow," she told Cass as she turned out the lamp. "I need my rest. I only hope I can sleep tonight. You know how I am before a big performance."

"Yes, I know. You can't sleep, so you can't resist keeping me up, too." Cass grinned at Suzette in the darkness. "At least I don't have to work tomorrow!"

The next morning, Suzette realized to her surprise that she had slept soundly.

"Now I know how to spend my off-day before performances," she said. "You've worked a miracle!"

Suzette began her preparations early for the opera. She had a pattern for the day that she had followed for every opera she'd sung for years. First she had a good breakfast with the usual coffee. Then she settled down to kill about six hours with Crawford movies. Since Suzette already knew them by heart, she would often doze during the films. She figured that that afforded her plenty of rest. Around four o'clock in the afternoon, she would do her usual stretches and meditation, careful to be thorough. Then a good dinner with plenty of protein, followed by a hot shower. Next Suzette listened to the opera in which she was currently performing. She wanted her role to be fresh in her mind. Finally, Suzette would go to the theater early to get into costume and make-up, leaving lots of time to warm up her voice.

Today's schedule followed the norm, except for one bit of excitement. Around two-thirty, in the middle of *A Woman's Face*, the doorbell rang.

"Do you want me to get that?" Cass called from upstairs where she lay reading.

"No, you needn't bother. I'm here already."

"Okay."

Suzette opened the door to discover an Express Mail carrier. She signed for the package, then looked around for a place to hide it.

"Who was it?" Cass called from the bedroom.

"Nobody," Suzette lied. "It was... Irene. She came to get her mop."

Suzette couldn't resist the temptation to open the package. She ducked behind the bar and ripped it open. From the torn wrappings Suzette drew a pale grey jewelers' box. She glanced at its contents, then quickly stashed the little box in the bar. Suzette caught herself grinning at odd moments throughout the rest of the afternoon. Cass had gone that morning to pick up her surprise. She brought it home swathed in paper and hung the bag in the wardrobe, making Suzette swear not to peek. Both women were excited about the long evening ahead.

At last Suzette left for the theater, after eating a fairly large dinner. Cass kissed her good-bye, saying "Break a leg, dear," in the tenderest of voices. She would meet Suzette backstage after the opera.

After Suzette left, Cass began her own preparations for the opera. As she carefully applied makeup and fixed her hair, she imagined Suzette doing the same. She could picture in her mind's eye Suzette putting her hair in pin-curls to go under her wig.

When Cass had showered and finished her face and hair, she brought out the surprise. She opened the wardrobe and removed the protective paper to reveal a glittering gown. Sliding the dress carefully over her head, Cass admired herself in the full-length mirror.

Indeed, Cass had much to admire. Various hues of green and gold threads were interwoven to create an indescribable fabric. The colors set off her flaming red hair to great advantage.

The gown was cut to cling, showing all Cass' shapely curves. The material fit snugly about her waist, blossoming outward at the top and bottom to allow for hips and breasts. Diamonds in gold dangled from her ears and sparkled at her throat. A gold clutch and shoes completed her formal attire.

When Cass was ready, she bundled up in the ankle-length mink she had brought for the occasion. She intended to sail into the opera in style.

Meanwhile, Suzette had dressed early. She remained in her dressing room, concentrating on relaxation. When she felt relaxed, Suzette began to focus her thoughts on the many characteristics of Octavian. Suzette embraced each one until at last she became Octavian. When she felt completely comfortable, Suzette left the dressing room and went out on stage. She strode about the Marschallin's boudoir in freedom for the last time, knowing that her next moves in that space would be in a pre-ordained pattern. Suzette wanted to capture the feel of the bedroom, of the imaginary scene before the opera begins.

The stage manager tapped her gently on the shoulder.

"Places," she whispered.

"Thank you." Octavian turned silently to take his place by the bed. Moments later the Marschallin joined him, climbing into the huge bed. But it wasn't the Marschallin who turned to Suzette and reached out to lightly stroke her fingertips over Suzette's cheek. The touch sent rivulets of ice water down Suzette's spine. Margaret's sweetest smile curled her lips and she whispered so that only Suzette could hear, "Time for bed again, dahling." Margaret let her fingers trail down Suzette's neck, over her shirt, and lingered with the briefest of touches on Suzette's left breast.

Margaret dropped her eyes with her hand, then raised them half way to look at Suzette. She smiled again, slowly, coldly.

Caught off-guard by the venom in Margaret's manner, Suzette froze, a reply caught in her throat. Then it was too late for speech. The two singers heard the

185

brass pronounce their opening call. Thirty seconds later, they heard the soft clank and whirr of the act curtain rising. Suzette's pulse beat faster as she rose up from the depths of the great bed to sing. She could feel the tangible presence of the audience. They seemed to breathe with her while she sang her floating raptures.

Suzette was enjoying herself immensely. She lived for such moments. To sing before an audience was her reason for living. It made the long rehearsals worth it—bad ones and good. The many hours she spent learning a new role were pleasure as well as work for Suzette, for she worked with that future audience in the back of her mind. As a result, Suzette always gave her best in performance.

Tonight was no exception. Suzette played the lightning-fast mood swings of an adolescent boy as though they were her own. From ardent love to indignation at the dawn, Octavian plunged boldly onward. But as Suzette sang rapturously from behind the giant bed, caressing the Marschallin's hand, Margaret grabbed Suzette's wrist and sat up. Startled, Suzette almost lost the flow of the song, but she didn't struggle in Margaret's grip. Margaret's eyes simmered with a viciousness utterly foreign to what the Marschallin was supposed to be feeling. Half by instinct, Suzette extended her arm, putting her body as far from Margaret as possible and bringing her, again, into the audience's view. After a time, Margaret gave up and released her.

She did that on purpose! thought Suzette. She was too shocked at Margaret's unprofessional behavior to realize that more surprises awaited her. When the bell signals the arrival of the morning's chocolate, Octavian runs behind the screen to hide. Instead of helping her lover, this Marschallin stepped directly into Octavian's path. Always quick on her feet, Suzette gave a little sideskip, pirouetted around Margaret, and gave her a quick peck on the cheek before hiding behind the screen.

After the servant leaves and Octavian comes back from behind the screen, the two sit down to a romantic breakfast. Romance, however, was a mood Suzette found it difficult to maintain. Images of Margaret as she had played the scene a few weeks earlier kept flashing unbidden through Suzette's head. Octavian reaches tenderly for the Marschallin's hand. Margaret moved her hand gracefully away, reaching for her chocolate. Suzette was left with no choice but to place her own hand on the tablecloth where Margaret's had been a moment before.

Octavian leans over to kiss the Marschallin a few minutes later, but Margaret turned her head so that all Suzette managed was a peck on the cheek. *She's sabotaging the scene*, thought Suzette. *It will be ridiculous if I'm is so restrained. After all, I'm supposed to have just spent the night with her.* But as Octavian reaches again for the Marschallin's hand, Margaret lifted her hand to pat her wig, leaving Suzette limp wristed in the air. *I'm not letting her get away with the coy maiden routine*, thought Suzette. *We're going to have some romance in this scene if it kills me.* Suzette slipped her arm around Margaret's waist and softly stroked her cheek. Margaret demured and tried to pull away, irritation showing in her eyes. Suzette held on tight, determined to appear affectionate.

Margaret looked anything but loving at the moment, her eyes smoldering. She knew if she pulled away forcefully, she would be completely out of character. The audience would know that something was wrong. Margaret had no choice this time. Defeated, she let herself go limp in Suzette's arms.

At last the love scene ends with the entrance of Baron Ochs, the Marschallin's cousin, come to plead the Marschallin's help in winning the hand of fifteen-year-old Sophie Faninal, whom he wants to marry for her money. Once more Octavian ducks behind the screen, to emerge as Mariandel, the Marschallin's serving girl. Suzette's eyes met Greg's. She was especially glad to see him, after the way Margaret had been acting. She didn't think Margaret's antics had been obvious to the audience, but she wondered if the rest of the cast had noticed.

The Baron reveals that he wants the Marschallin to send Sophie an emissary with a silver rose. The Marschallin shows him a portrait of her "cousin," Octavian, saying he is of royal blood. The Baron is delighted. Count Octavian merely giggles in his skirts.

The rest of the act moved along without a hitch. The Marschallin sends away the Baron, Octavian, and the rest of the motley crew that formed her entourage. Alone, she recalls the days of her youth, when she was a bride fresh out of the convent, just as Sophie Faninal is now. She muses on the passage of time and the loss of her youth. Margaret was in her element. Though she may have been past her prime, she could still sing beautifully, her long notes floating suspended overhead like wisps of clouds. The audience was rapt, not a cough or a rustle to be heard. Margaret let a tear creep into her voice, wringing the hearts of her audience, making them hers.

Act II went smoothly without Margaret in it. Octavian arrives to deliver the rose, and he and Sophie fall in love, as they are supposed to. Both Suzette and Jennifer were able to recapture the sense of infatuation they had found so many rehearsals ago when they had only an old screwdriver to represent the rose. Tonight, however, their surroundings reflect the grand and noble emotions pouring forth in the music. The two women molded music and setting into a thing of complete beauty— absolute perfection.Unfortunately, the Baron arrives to settle his alliance with Sophie, but his lecherous advances and boorish manners disgust her.

Octavian picks a quarrel and wounds the Baron in the arm as they fight. Sophie declares she will not marry the Baron or anyone else. Her father threatens to send her to a convent forever if she doesn't change her mind.

Octavian realizes he must outwit the Baron if he is to prevent this marriage. The second act ends with Herr Faninal supporting the Baron's claims, and the Baron receiving a note from Mariandel setting up an assignation with him in an inn.

Cass left her box at the second intermission to get something to drink. She saw the Thayers in the hallway and made her way over to them.

"Hello, Irene, Joseph," Cass said. "I'm glad you decided to come. Suzette told me you might."

Irene was delighted to see her. "Hello, dear. I'm glad we came, too. Your friend sings beautifully."

"Thank you." Cass couldn't help beaming with pride. "Personally, I would have to say that Suzette's my favorite opera singer."

"You two girls are such good friends— do you hear her often?" Irene inquired.

Cass smiled broadly. "As often as I can."

Joseph cleared his throat. "Excuse me, ladies, but I believe they have signaled for us to take our seats."

"I'm glad I saw you. I'll be sure and tell Suzette that you came," Cass said as they split up and went back to their seats.

Cass drummed her fingers on the arm of her chair. She had seen the tricks Margaret played on Suzette during Act I. Cass was proud of Suzette for her lightning-quick recoveries, but Act III worried her.

Cass was definitely ready for the opera to be over. She shuddered to think that Suzette would have to deal with the party after such a challenging onstage bout with Margaret. How well would she hold up through the rest of the evening? Cass knew that later they would both have to give the performance of their lives.

Silence fell as a spotlight pinpointed the conductor. Maestro Kleinemann took a bow, then bade his orchestra rise. When the applause finally died down, he lifted his baton and began. The curtain rose with the opening strains of the act to reveal the inside of an inn.

The group that Octavian has hired to make a fool of the Baron succeeds well. As he attempts to seduce Mariandel, faces appear from panels, men pop out of trapdoors, a woman rushes in claiming to be his wife, and strange children call him "Papa." He begins to doubt his reason. The commissary of police arrives to arrest him on a charge of leading young girls astray. At first he claims Mariandel is Sophie, but Herr Faninal and Sophie show up to disprove that lie. Faninal is furious as the Baron's true character is revealed, and Sophie renounces him. Mariandel disappears behind the bed curtains to shed her skirts.

Then Margaret entered as the Marschallin.

Octavian wants to know why the Marschallin is there. He pops his head out of the curtains to ask. As soon as Suzette appeared, Margaret whirled to face her. Margaret swung her hand high, bringing it down in a resounding slap. Suzette's face burned from the blow. Flinging open the curtains, she stood revealed as Octavian.

Fortunately, at that moment a wave of creditors appears to bear the Baron offstage. The confusion allowed Suzette time to recover her composure. *Enough is enough. That bitch is going to pay.* Suzette very calmly and coldly began the final scene. Suzette saw Margaret's smug, satisfied smile. She evidently now felt free to give herself to her last aria. She sang of the misuse of time and men, once again spinning out her silver tones. Suzette waited until Margaret became totally involved in her aria then gently reached out and took both of her hands, as if in friendship. Margaret continued singing, aware only of her voice. She didn't realize that Suzette had delicately pulled her around until she was singing directly into the wings. Her last glorious song was directed at the stagehands. She became aware of her position only when she heard the slightly puzzled applause of the audience. She was furious, but it was too late to do anything more to Suzette, as Octavian and Sophie pledge their love, and Margaret was compelled to give the Marschallin's blessing to Sophie. The opera ends happily for all but the Marschallin. And Margaret.

Chapter 17

Suzette was elated. She bounced in place behind the great door as she waited for her curtain call. She was the last to take a bow. When she ran out through the big inn door, the applause was deafening. Suzette couldn't stop grinning. Finally, after several curtain calls, the cast was able to leave the stage. Suzette rushed to her dressing room to change. As she burst into the hallway behind the stage, she saw Cass waiting for her at the door to her dressing room. Cass looked so stunning in her evening gown that Suzette stopped short. She recovered quickly, though, and bounded down the hall to meet her lover.

"Haven't gotten out of character yet, have you?" Cass remarked as Suzette stopped, breathless.

Suzette grinned sheepishly. "I guess not. Would you care to come in?"

"Most definitely," Cass replied as she followed Suzette into the tiny room. "Need help changing?"

"No, but you know how I am. I just want you in here because I'm such an exhibitionist."

"You certainly proved that tonight, but it was well worth it. You were wonderful, love." Cass leaned over to kiss Suzette on the cheek. "Here," she said, handing Suzette a large bundle. "What's opening night without flowers?"

"What, indeed!" Suzette laughed as she added the flowers from Cass to her already large collection. "I'll put yours in front where I can see them. I have something for you, too, you know. That little surprise I was telling you about."

Cass was still dying with curiosity. "Where is it? Can I have it now?"

"Just wait a little while longer, till I'm dressed. Go see if you can find Fred. He'd love to hear what you thought of the opera, I know." Suzette finished unpinning her wig. "I've got to take a shower before we go."

"I know that will take a while," Cass laughed. "Maybe I will go find Fred."

Cass went off to find Fred, who was in the green room talking to various patrons of the opera who had come backstage to see the stars. He was glad to get taken away from them by Cass. The two of them escaped to the coffee vending machines downstairs.

"It will take Susie awhile to get dressed," Cass mentioned to Fred.

"Yes, I imagine it will." *Even longer than you think.* Fred thought to himself. *Especially since I promised to keep you here until the house cleared out.*

They chattered about the evening's performance, then wandered on to other upcoming projects. Finally Fred decided that enough time had passed.

"Let's go back upstairs," Fred suggested. "I want to show you something."

Cass agreed, and followed Fred willingly back up to the stage. She began to get suspicious when he led her out onto the set. The stage had been reset for Act II, which struck Cass as being very odd. The sensible thing to do would be to set up Act I for the next performance.

"What kind of mischief are you up to, Fred?" Cass asked.

"Just wait and see. I think you'll like it." Fred smiled. "Now sit down here. I have to get something."

Cass sat obediently in the large, graceful chair that Fred had pointed out. She didn't have to wait long before the great double doors swung wide. Through them came Jennifer Doyle carrying a small black box.

"Hello. I'm..."

"Jennifer Doyle," Cass finished for her. "I've heard so much about you! It's a pleasure to meet you."

"Thank you." Jennifer smiled. The compliments from Cass were obviously genuine. Jennifer held out the small box. "This is for you, from Suzette."

"Thank you." Cass took the box from Jennifer's outstretched hand. "Won't you have a seat?"

"I'm afraid I have to run. I'll be seeing you at the ball, though, I understand. We can talk more there."

"Well, at least stay to see what's in the package. Aren't you curious? I certainly am," Cass grinned.

Jennifer hesitated. Deciding, she sat down in the chair beside Cass. "You're right. I'm dying to see what she brought you!"

Cass and Jennifer leaned closer together as Cass opened the velvet case. There, lying nestled in the soft black cloth, lay an intricately wrought platinum watch fob. Cass gently lifted it out of the box, holding it up to the light. She traced the fine work with her eyes, going over every petal of the tiny filigree rose set into the middle of the fob. A single diamond sparkled from the heart of the rose like a drop of morning dew.

"It's beautiful," Jennifer whispered. Cass was speechless.

"Do you like it, Cass?" Suzette had been standing unseen in the doorway for a couple of minutes.

Cass jumped up and went to throw her arms around Suzette's neck. "Like it? I love it!" Cass gave Suzette a quick kiss. "Wherever did you get it?"

"I had a friend of mine make it for you. She'd already designed the rose, or she couldn't have finished in time. Now let's go to the ball!" Suzette squeezed Cass' hand. "We've got quite an evening ahead."

Jennifer took her leave of the happy couple. "I'll see you there. 'Bye!"

Fred walked on stage just as Jennifer left. "So what do you think of your surprise?"

"It's beautiful... and so appropriately presented!" Cass laughed. "But no one's said anything about the surprise I brought!"

Suzette was dismayed. "Oh, darling, you look positively ravishing. I'm sorry that I didn't say something sooner. You know, when I first saw you in the corridor outside my dressing room, why, you literally took my breath away." Suzette looked Cass up and down appreciatively. "Cass bought this new gown just for tonight," she explained to Fred. "She wouldn't let me see it before the opera."

"You two women had better hurry up, then , and get to the party. It would be a shame to waste such a fabulous gown." Fred smiled. "You look pretty sharp, yourself, Suzette."

"Let's go in my car, Cass. We can pick yours up tomorrow."

"All right. We'll see you there, Fred."

When the two women had folded themselves into Suzette's small car, Cass leaned over for a more lingering kiss.

"I do love your dress, love," Suzette whispered as she traced the exposed line of Cass' breast with her fingertip. "Maybe we should forget the party and just go home. I wouldn't mind examining your outfit a bit more closely."

Cass laughingly pushed Suzette aside. "Come on, we'll have plenty of time to play around later. How many times have I been invited to the Grand Ball at the C.O.C.?"

"Okay, okay. But remember, you promised to dance with me tonight."

"Believe me, I would never forget such a promise." Cass kissed Suzette one last time, before Suzette started the car.

They had soon driven the short distance to the ballroom. "Shall we go inside in style?" Suzette asked as she offered Cass her arm.

"But of course," Cass replied, wrapping her hand around Suzette's elbow.

"Well, here goes," Suzette said, taking a deep breath. I'm more nervous than I was for the opera."

"That's understandable," Cass assured her. "This may be a more important performance."

When the two women walked through the ballroom door, they were surprised by a thunderous round of applause. Cass stepped back to allow Suzette her moment. When the party resumed its dull roar and Suzette was no longer the center of attention, Cass rejoined her lover.

"Why didn't you stay with me?" Suzette asked.

"You deserved that applause. I didn't want to detract from your glory. After all, you were the star of the evening," Cass replied. "Besides, the night is young. There's plenty of time to make trouble together. And I also thought that we were going to be tasteful about creating this situation."

"You're so right. Oh, sweetheart, I love you so."

"I love you, too, darling. Now let's get some champagne and celebrate your debut!"

The two women took drinks from a passing waiter, then began to mingle. They stayed close to each other at first, with Suzette introducing Cass to the other cast and crew members.

"There's Jennifer," said Suzette. "You've met her already."

"Yes, *your* rose bearer," smiled Cass. Jennifer spotted them at the same time and made her way over.

"Did you come alone?" asked Cass.

"Yes, I'm not as brave as the two of you. Speaking of brave, there's Miss Guerrilla Warfare hanging on her husband's arm."

Suzette turned to look in the direction Jennifer had indicated. She hesitated for a second, then decisively waved Margaret over.

"Why did you do that?" Jennifer asked, wide-eyed, as Cass stared in amazement. "She stabbed you in the back all evening. It's a wonder you're still alive."

"I still have to work with her," Suzette replied. "Anyway, I think she got out all her frustrations on-stage."

"She doesn't look like she did," Cass muttered.

Indeed she didn't. Margaret whispered something to her husband and released his arm, baring her fangs as she glided across the room towards Suzette.

Before she could say anything, though, Suzette decided to take the situation firmly in hand. "Margaret, I would like to introduce you to my lover, Cassandra Kelley. Cass, this is Margaret Byrd."

"Hello, Suzette," Margaret said, brushing past Cass as though she weren't there. "You were marvelous, Suzette dahling. Almost as good a performance as the private one you gave me. I never had a chance to thank you properly for that one."

"It was nothing," Suzette said, holding Margaret's eyes with hers for a moment, "Really nothing." Then she brushed past Margaret with her eyes as Margaret had just done to Cass.

"May I have this dance?" she asked, turning to Cass.

"I would be delighted." Jennifer smiled and Margaret glared as Cass and Suzette left to work their way through the crowd toward the dance floor. Several songs went by before they were able to dance, however. Suzette kept bumping into people she knew. Cass accepted the diversions as inevitable.

Suzette saw Maestro Kleinemann and introduced Cass to him. The esteemed conductor shook hands with Cass, beaming over his shoulder at Suzette.

"She is something, this Fraulein," he said to Cass. "A beautiful, beautiful voice. You see that she takes care of it, ja?"

Cass smiled and nodded at him before she was pulled in another direction.

"Cass, I want you to meet Gregory Loft. Gregory, this is my spouse, Cassandra Kelley." Suzette had steered Cass up to the tall, graceful man who had, just a few hours earlier, had been a bumbling oaf.

"A pleasure." Gregory's handshake was good and solid. "Fred's told me so much about you."

"Oh, he has, has he?" Cass was taken aback. Suzette, however, assessed the situation correctly.

"I'll explain later, darling. Gregory, you'll have to come to dinner with us sometime soon."

"I would like that. Now if you'll pardon me, I must get back to my wife."

When Gregory had disappeared into the crowd, Cass put a firm hand on Suzette's arm. "What in the world was that all about?"

"My hunch is that Gregory Loft is the singer that Fred's been seeing," Suzette whispered. "I imagine he got away from us so quickly to cover his own tracks."

"I understand," Cass whispered back. "The other gays in the room don't want to be found guilty by association. It seems the heteros are more likely to befriend us."

"So it seems, indeed." Suzette no longer whispered. "Now, how about that dance?"

The two women had finally reached the dance floor, Cass discovered when she glanced behind herself. "As I said before, I would love to dance." She gladly took Suzette's arm. "You'd better lead tonight, dear. After all, you've had plenty of practice at being the butch this evening."

Suzette took Cass in her arms and began to waltz. She felt self-conscious at first, but soon the surreptitious stares of bystanders became less frequent. After a few turns around the dance floor Suzette was able to ignore the other party-goers and concentrate on the beautiful woman she held, the woman who gracefully followed Suzette's slightest whim.

Cass was enjoying herself immensely. She loved to waltz, because it was the closest she had ever come to wingless flight. Cass couldn't remember the last time she and Suzette had had the opportunity for ballroom dancing. On the rare occasions when they had gone dancing in the past few years, it had been to dark smoky bars filled with women dancing to rock or disco or new wave or, as in one instance, reggae.

The next dance the band played was a polka.

"Let's stay!" Cass was eager for more dancing.

"All right." Suzette was having a good time, too, and didn't require much encouragement to continue.

The two of them whirled around the floor through dance after dance. When the band finally stopped for a break, the women were breathless. Suzette steered Cass to a chair by one wall.

"Cass, you've met Barb, the stagemanager. She seems to be the only crew member here tonight. Why don't you visit while I go for more champagne and hors d'oeuvres?" With that, Suzette disappeared, leaving Cass to her own devices.

Barb leaned close to Cass. "You know, I suspected you from the minute I met you. I must say, you and Miss Etoile are awfully brave, coming here together as though it was the most natural thing in the world."

"Well, it is the most natural thing in the world, if you think about it. We love each other, we live together, we do everything we can together—why not be here tonight together? It seems more unnatural for me to stay home, somehow." Cass grinned. "I almost wish we'd done this years ago."

"Why 'almost'?"

"You know, I'm sure. When being different is frowned upon by society, people who are different in some way are driven underground. You said we were brave. Lots of people are probably thinking we're stupid." Cass sighed. "I don't even know whether or not this is crazy. But if it is crazy, at least we had more than five years of relative peace."

"You seem to be doing okay so far," Barb said, surveying the crowd. "No riots yet. Say, didn't you tell me you were a techie?"

"Why, yes, in fact I am. I'm the designer and technical director at a small college." Cass plunged into a description of the project she had just finished. She and Barb both were delighted to have found someone who spoke their own language.

Suzette bumped into Fred on her way to find food and drink. "How are we doing?" she whispered.

"I've been hearing more about your onstage performance than your offstage one, so I'd say pretty good." Fred paused to munch on a canapé before continuing. "The general consensus seems to be live and let live. Almost everyone seems to intend to ignore you unless directly confronted."

"Well, I've confronted several, already, but I haven't received anything worse than a cold shoulder. And

that was from Margaret, which was the least I expected from her!" Suzette picked up a plate of food and a
couple of glasses of champagne. "I'll keep you posted
if you'll do the same for me."

"You've got it," Fred replied just before Suzette
disappeared into the throng.

Suzette had just rejoined Cass and Barb when she
saw Margaret heading toward her with another woman in tow.

"Now what?" Suzette managed to whisper to Cass
just before Margaret sallied up to them.

"Hello, dahling." Margaret's voice was as slick as oil
on water. "I have someone I'd like you to meet. Mrs.
Vandegelder, this is Suzette Etoile, our Count Octavian. Suzette, this is Mrs. Vandegelder. She writes for
the social register, and covers these soirées for the
Times. I know the two of you have ever so much to discuss, so I'll just leave you alone." Almost before she
finished her introductions, Margaret Byrd was gone.

"Good evening, dear. It really is a pleasure to meet
you. I enjoyed the opera immensely, especially you,
my dear. Didn't you have a simply fabulous time playing a man?"

Suzette was a bit surprised by this outburst, but
was determined to keep her cool. "Thank you. Yes, I
did enjoy myself quite a bit. This is the first time I've
played a pants role, you know."

"No, I didn't realize. I'm surprised. You seemed so
natural on stage," Mrs. Vandegelder replied.

"That's because I'm an actress as well as a singer,
Mrs. Vandegelder," Suzette said before the woman
could squeeze in another question. "Allow me to introduce my partner, Cassandra Kelley, and our stagemanager, Barb..."

"Furles," Barb finished for her. "Barbara Furles.
It's a pleasure to meet you."

"The same, I'm sure," Mrs. Vandegelder said quickly before turning to Cass. "You must be very proud of your friend."

Cass wasn't quite sure how to deal with this woman, so she opted for honesty coupled with brevity. "Yes, I am," was all she said.

"You don't have to be shy with me, dear," Mrs. Vandegelder said reassuringly, patting Cass' hand. "So lovely... you remind me of a very dear old friend of mine. She's dead now, poor dear."

"Oh?" Suzette's curiosity was captured.

"Yes, indeed. She was my best friend—lovely, like you," Mrs. Vandegelder continued, "with the same remarkable red hair. Now don't get me wrong. You two young ladies should find nice young men and get married. But take my advice: Never let them come between you. Husbands are merely a necessary convenience, you know." Mrs. Vandegelder laughed. "Here I am, doing all the talking. I do ramble on so. Oh, there's that handsome Mr. Loft. Excuse me, dears, I do so want to meet him."

As she made her her way through the crowd, Mrs. Vandegelder was unaware of the amusement she had left in her wake. Suzette, Cass and Barb tried vainly to stifle their laughter, but only succeeded in reducing themselves to a fit of the giggles.

"Do you think she was for real?" Barb asked.

"Of course. And to think Margaret thought she was throwing me to the wolves! If only she knew," Suzette managed to say between bouts of laughter. "She would be horrified. So much for my first exposure in the media as a lesbian!"

"Yes," Cass added, "She'll probably just list you among the 'people who attended' as Miss Suzette Etoile the brilliant singer and her friend, Miss Cassandra Kelley."

Suzette agreed. "I would be very surprised to see anything more. She sounded like a benevolent closet case to me."

By now the three women had calmed down somewhat. Barb raised her glass high. "I would like to propose a toast. To our invisible family."

"May they become visible," Suzette added.

Cass clinked her glass to theirs. "I'll drink to that."

The rest of the evening proved relatively uneventful. Cass and Suzette danced until they thought their feet would never live to see the light of day. Once they had gotten over their initial discomfort at the party, they had a grand time. Finally, in the wee hours of the morning, Suzette and Cass headed for home.

"Looks like we closed the place down," Cass remarked as they left. Suzette surveyed the wreckage of the nearly empty ballroom as she nodded in agreement.

When the two women reached the car, Suzette opened and held the car door for Cass. "I've been playing butch all evening," she laughed. "Why stop now? Here's my chance to prove chivalry is not dead!"

Suzette's adrenaline continued to flow until after they reached the apartment. She was high on champagne and a feeling of victory.

"What a team we are," Suzette whispered excitedly as she unzipped the shimmering green-gold gown for Cass, running one fingertip down her long, smooth back.

"You're right about that," Cass said as she turned to kiss her lover. "Let's keep it that way."

"It's a deal. Now slide your gorgeous body out of that gown and come to bed with me."

"Yes, ma'am," Cass said as she willingly complied.

When Cass had snuggled up next to her, Suzette sighed. "Suddenly I know what it really means to be tired." The long day, the intensity of the performance, and the excitement and anxiety of the ball had finally caught up with her.

"You've worked hard today," Cass whispered soothingly. "I'm very proud of you."

"Are you really?"

"Yes, I am. You gave a brilliant performance both onstage and off. I believe you've succeeded in what you set out to do. We were not kicked out of the Grand Ball for dancing together, and there was no indication that there will be major repercussions in your career because you have a female lover, either. I'm proud, and I also love you very much."

"There may still be rough weather ahead, but I don't want to turn back. We've come so far together—and I couldn't have done it without you." Suzette kissed Cass tenderly. "I love you, sweetheart. Sleep well tonight."

"You're right not to turn back, Susie. You're on the right track." Cass gazed lovingly at Suzette, already asleep beside her. She reached over and turned out the lamp, letting darkness fill the room. The last spark of light shone from Gertie's watchful eye as she sat at the foot of the bed, guardian of love's sweet sleep.